Hail Taushree

Making of RJCW Team

BY

Chhedi Singh Rangwala

Hail Taushree

First Published in March 2022

ISBN: 978-93-5611-558-3

BLUEROSE PUBLISHERS

www.bluerosepublishers.com

info@bluerosepublishers.com

+91 8882 898 898

Cover Design: Yashpal Singh

Distributed by: BlueRose, Amazon, Flipkart

Preface

Hail Taushree is a funny take on working culture of Indian Lala companies which are run like a provision store by their owners.

This story provides insight of how so called rich owners deal with key employees of their companies and resulting work culture in companies.

It may seem funny but this is the real truth of communications done by these owners with their key employees and how those key employees react to it.We have added bit (more!) of spice from our side to make it enjoyable while reading.

Sole purpose of this book is to induce laughter and a give overall idea of how these companies run. If we hurt someone (especially my own Taushree!!) with this book, please take my sincere apologies in advance.

All characters, events and company name are imaginary and if anything matches with anything even then we are fine with it so enjoy! Anyone who works in big lala company directly under their owners would be able to relate to it.

Story revolves around Mr.Taushree an extremely egoistic and self centric person. He is the owner of company named Mera Ego Limited. His company manufactures high end luxury shoes for overseas customers under the brand name “Kachra shoes”. One fine day he decides to create a new team of product scientists to bring revolutionary design changes in his company shoes. His decision results into creation of RJCW department and bringing Mahesh Chhedi, Atom Singh & Suresh Rangwala in the company.

Making of RJCW team story is about how above gentleman’s were interviewed, hired and the way they adjusted to working under Taushree.

CONTENTS

Weekend Fun 6
Interview of Mahesh Chhedi 17
Interview of Suresh Rangwala 25
The RJCW Department...36
Atom Singh:Marketing Expert 45
RJCW Team: Up & Running 53
Chugli the trouble maker 62
The Presentation 66
Atom Singh vs Chamcha Prasad 81
The Review..93
Suresh is Angry 98
Egoistic pig & his sycophant piglets 105

Weekend Fun

It's a nice and sunny sunday morning in Mumbai; Taushree is sitting in sky garden of his 29th floor penthouse thinking about improvements he can bring in Mera Ego Limited products and ways to screw up weekend of his employees. He decides to hire a team of new product scientists, He call his Vice President Mr.Pedaishi Gulam and Director Mr.Chamcha Prasad.

Taushree on call with Pediashi Gulam & Chamcha Prasad : Pedaishi Gulam , to introduce new designs of Kachra shoes to our customers in Europe I want to hire a team of top class product scientists with overseas experience for our office in Mumbai , Salary no bar.I will personally interview everyone. I want to take at least 2 interviews tomorrow. Chamcha Prasad Ji, make sure to follow-up with Pedaishi Gulam and confirm this will be done tomorrow.

Although real meaning of above golden words from Taushree was " Mr.Pedaishi Gulam in last 20 years I have satisfied my ego by telling you and your team every moment that you all are fools and I have done you all favour by keeping you all and paying salary to all of you. Now I want to up my game and I want more experts with stronger technical background to prove my point and to prove to all those new experts that they are all fools". Reason for including Chamcha Prasad in this conversation was to make sure Chamcha Prasad's weekend also gets screwed up along with weekend of Pedaishi Gulam and his team.

Pedaishi Gulam to Taushree: Good morning Sir. Consider it done.

Chamcha Prasad to Taushree: Sorry but I must say sir, you are a visionary .This is exactly what we need to do to increase our revenue in such a challenging market.

Taushree to Chamcha Prasad: Chamcha ji , You see I am even working on weekend to increase our revenue.

Chamcha Prasad to Taushree: Sir, You are the one man army of Mera Ego Limited.

Taushree to Pedaishi Gulam: Pedaishi Gulam , I hope you have also understood how important this is for us so no excuses.. Tomorrow means tomorrow.

Pedaishi Gulam: Yes Sir.

Pedaishi Gulam calls his assistant Naukri Bachao Khan and asks him to find two people for interview tomorrow and tells him that Chamcha Prasad is also overlooking this task.Pediashi Gulam also mentioned to Naukri Bachao Khan that person called for interview should be best of the available talent pool available in industry.

Naukri Bachao Khan: Sir it will be done.

Now Naukri Bachao Khan was thinking how to get two best talents from industry for interview tomorrow. Understood that there is a huge possibility that Taushree will reject them all after taking their interview just to show Pedaishi Gulam, Chamcha Prasad and whole team that they can't find even a single decent person for company. But as task is given it has to be done.

Naukri Bachao Khan and team pulled out all the resumes from company database and started doing cold calling to all prospective candidates but no one was ready to come for interview next day.

Naukri Bachao Khan: Chugli bhai ,boss will fire us, any suggestions?

Chugli Kumar:Naukri Bachao Sir.. Let's find an unemployed expert.

Naukri Bachao Khan: Chugli what if boss came to know we deliberately tried to find unemployed person instead of highly sought out best talents or if somebody did a chugli to get some extra points from boss?

Chugli Kumar: Naukri Bachao Sir who will tell, it's between you & me .We need to save our jobs, as my boss you need to take decision.

Meanwhile Taushree again called Pedaishi Gulam & Chamcha Prasad and reminded them that he wants to take interview tomorrow at any cost.

Taushree : Pedaishi Gulam Ji & Chamcha Prasad Ji , I hope you understand that situation is very critical. Please don't sleep over it; I need product scientists in my office tomorrow. Update me on progress every hour.

Pedaishi Gulam to Taushree: Sir both the pillars of company Naukri & Chugli are on this along with me.

Taushree to Pedaishi Gulam: Ask Chugli to update me also. His updates are very satisfactory.

Pedaishi Gulam calls Naukri Bachao Khan and Chugli Kumar to get updates.

Pedaishi Gulam: Naukri & Chugli any updates.

Naukri Bachao Khan to Pediashi Gulam: Gulam sir, We are trying our best to arrange interview for tomorrow but nobody is ready to come for interview tomorrow.

Pedaishi Gulam: Naukri & Chugli this needs to be done today itself , instructions from Mr.Taushree are very clear we need experts in our office tomorrow for interview. Chugli , Mr.Taushree has asked you to update him on progress.

Chugli to Pedaishi Gulam: I will update him every 30mins.

It was clear that it's next to impossible to find a good candidate for interview next day so both Naukri and Chugli started to make their own strategy. Naukri was thinking if we can get any unemployed candidate for interview next day as suggested by Chugli and Chugli was thinking how to get extra points from top boss and also screw up his immediate boss Naukri Bachao in a one go.

Naukri Bachao pulled out the list of candidates actively seeking employment and started calling them.

Naukri Bachao called first candidate Dharambir Berozgaar.

Naukri Bachao: Mr. Dharambir Berozgaar , I am calling from Mera Ego Limited. We are a major shoe manufacturers based in Mumbai. We manufacture luxury shoes for European market. We have a position for a product scientist in our Mumbai office. Are you interested?

Dharambir Berozgaar: Mera Ego Limited! Sorry, I heard from my friends that owner of company is a crazy person; He treats his employees as his slaves.I will find it hard to cope up with such a person.

Dharambir Berozgaar hangs up the phone.

Naukri Bachao Khan discussing with Chugli Kumar: Chugli even unemployed person refused saying our owner is crazy.

He is company owner not our owner replied Chugli Kumar.Why don't you tell him that he will be a part of technical team and will never be interacting with company owner.

Naukri Bachao Khan again calls Dharambir Berozgaar: Mr.Berozgaar, see you will be a part of technical team and you will be never interacting with company owner.So you don't need to worry about company owner's nature.

If company treats me with dignity then Sure I am interested replied Dharambir Berozgaar.

Naukri Bachao Khan: So tomorrow you have to come for interview in our Mumbai office.

Dharambir Berozgaar: Sir tomorrow it's not possible. I am at my in-laws house in Pune. Any reason why it's so urgent?

Naukri Bachao Khan: Actually our owner wants to take your interview tomorrow.

OWNER! What? You just said I will be a part of technical team so I will not be interacting with owner of company! Asked Dharambir Berozgaar in a surprised tone.

Naukri Bachao Khan correcting himself: No its just owner takes interview of new joiner and after that you will be a part of technical team and will not be interacting with owner.

Dharambir Berozgaar: Alright, but It will be not feasible for me to present in Mumbai tomorrow, I am in Pune at present.

Naukri Bachao Khan: No issues please take Pune to Mumbai taxi, we will reimburse.

Dharambir Berozgaar: Alright I will come tomorrow morning.

Chugli Kumar was listening to all the conversation and he immediately knew that there is a scope to screw up Naukri Bachao khan.

To provide updates Chugli Kumar called Taushree .

Chugli Kumar to Taushree: Good morning sir, I am calling you to provide updates on arrangement for tomorrow interview.

Taushree to Chugli Kumar: Hold on Chugli let me take Pedaishi Gulam and Chamcha Prasad ji on call also.

Now it's conference call between Taushree , Chugli Kumar , Pedaishi Gulam & Chamcha Prasad.

Chugli Kumar: Naukri Bachao sir has arranged an interview with Mr.Dharambir Berozgaar.As Naukri sir is not able to convince already employed candidates to work for us, he called Mr.Dharambir Berozgaar. Dharambir Berozgaar is currently unemployed.In addition to fixing an interview Naukri sir has also promised Mr.Berozgaar reimbursement of taxi charges from Pune to Mumbai.

Now Taushree was furious from outside but extremely happy from inside as he just got a very interesting point to screw up Naukri Bachao and his boss Pedaishi Gulam.

Taushree added Naukri Bachao khan also on conference call.

Naukri Bachao Khan in conference call: Good morning Taushree sir.

Taushree to Naukri Bachao Khan: Good morning Naukri Bachao. How is search going on?

Naukri Bachao Khan to Taushree: Sir, its going great we just fixed an interview of Mr.Dharambir Berozgaar.

Taushree: Naukri where Mr.Berozgaar works.

Naukri: Sir, currently he is unemployed.

Taushree: So I asked you to get the best talent and you found an unemployed person to waste my time!

Now Taushree was Yelling at Pedaishi Gulam , **You and Naukri are good for nothing.I should have fired you both long ago , but still I chose to keep you guys and pay useless person such as you and Naukri such a huge salary.I am feeding your families and instead of working for me honestly you guys are trying to make fool of me!**

Chamcha Prasad intervened.

Chamcha Prasad: Naukri Bachao how can you do this with us. You should have some sincerity towards Mera Ego Limited. See Mr.Taushree is taking so much pain even on weekend in chalking out growth plan and strategy to increase company revenue.I have observed that in last 5 years our revenune is not growing despite having Mr.Taushree who is the most intelligent person in this unverse on top of us.Now I have reached the conclusion its because of person like you who is not helping us in implementing Taushree's plan.

Even before Naukri replies to anything, Chugli Kumar jumped in:

Chugli Kumar: As Taushree Sir has said we need to get best talent and unemployed persons are not needed, let me call Dharambir Berozgaar and tell him interview is cancelled otherwise he will come and we will have to pay him to & fro taxi fare from Pune to Mumbai.

Although this was not needed from Chugli Kumar but now all hell broke loose.Anger of Taushree was on highest part of heaven and all those heavenly goodies were bound to fall on Naukri Bachao Khan and his immediate supervisor Pedaishi Gulam. Getting an unemployed candidate for interview and also paying taxi fare to him!!!

This time Taushree kept his cool and asked Pedaishi Gulam to scold Naukri Bachao Khan.

Taushree: Everyone should learn from Pediashi Gulam how to cut the tree you are sitting in!! Everyone tell me loud what you should learn from Mr.Pediashi Gulam?

Everyone in conference call started shouting:how to cut the tree you are sitting in!

Once everyone was done , Taushree again started talking with Pedaishi Gulam.

Taushree to Pediashi Gulam: Pedaishi Gulam , do you know why I made everbody shout those golden words for you?

No Sir replied Pedaishi Gulam

Taushree: Because I am paying you and your team salary to help me in doing few small things for company and you and your team have completely failed in doing it. Instead of feeling shame on your failure you and Naukri Bachao Khan are doing stupid things.Tell me why should I pay salary to you and Naukri Bachao Khan?

Pedaishi Gulam was very clear now Taushree wanted Pedaishi Gulam to scold Naukri Bachao Khan and praise Taushree

Pedaishi Gulam to Naukri Bachao Khan: Naukri Bachao Can't you see Taushree is working so hard to make sure Mera Ego limited succeeds and it is the responsibility of each one of us to make sure company succeeds by implementing growth plan of Taushree properly. However instead of trying to make this happen you are trying to fool all of us .It does not works like this, if you can't please tell us. We can easily find your replacement after firing you.

Naukri Bacho Khan thinking idea of getting unemployed expert was from Chugli Kumar but why everyone is abusing me? Leave it just say sorry and finish it of.

Naukri Bachao Khan to Pedaishi Gulam: Sorry sir, this will not be repeated.

Taushree to Naukri Bachao Khan: Naukri Bachao, Your salary for this month is on hold if you didn't get candidate for me tomorrow. Pedaishi Gulam ask Mota Rancho to hold Naukri Bachao Salary and company will pay Chugli 10,000 rupees as bonus for being sincere to company and bringing up this important issue to management.

Mota Rancho is finance manager of Mera Ego Limited.

Naukri Bachao Khan now knew that he is in trouble and there is no way out, He will not be able to find a person for tomorrow meeting and his salary will be on hold. Further he needs to find a person for interview with Taushree as soon as possible and after that cry in front of Taushree to get his salary. In simple words Naukri Bachao was clear now he will have to do lots of shit clean work just to satisfy ego of Taushree in coming days.

Pedaishi Gulam and Naukri Bachao did cold calling whole day on sunday just to have someone for interview. While Chugli Kumar was not doing anything, his job was just to call Taushree every 30 minutes and do as much back biting as possible.

Interview of Mahesh Chhedi

Next day monday morning everyone was in office and there was no candidate for interview.

Taushree was frantically abusing whole of the team and Naukri Bachao was frantically calling all the prospective candidates for interview that to without any travelling allowance. Whereas Pediashi Gulam took the responsibility of facing the wrath of Taushree and satisfy the ego of Taushree.

Finally Naukri Bachao Khan managed to convience one good candidate for interview next week Mr.Mahesh Chhedi. Mr.Chhedi is one of the best luxury shoe designer available in industry. His expertise is in formal shoe with designer hole in front.

Telephonic discussion between Naukri Bachao Khan and Mahesh Chhedi was interesting:

Naukri Bachao Khan: Mr.Mahesh Chhedi, I am calling from Mera Ego Limited .We are looking for talented product designer for our Kachra Shoe Brand.

Mahesh Chhedi: Mera Ego Limited, Glassdoor says it's better to commit sucide than to join Mera Ego Limited.

Mahesh Chhedi hangs up the phone but Naukri Bachao Khan tired of getting same answers from all prospective candidates and desparate to get out of this mess calls back Mahesh Chhedi.

Naukri Bachao Khan: Mr.Chhedi these are just romuors flying around our company.You will be a part of technical team and will never be interacting with owner of company. You will interact with company owner only during your interview.More than that we are open to big salary negotiations.

Mahesh Chhedi: Alright , I will come for interview.

D-Day arrives and Mr.Chhedi comes to office of Mera Ego Limited for interview with Mr.Taushree. Naukri Bachao Khan took him directly to Cabin of Taushree.In that cabin Pedaishi Gulam and Chamcha Prasad were already present.

Mahesh Chhedi: Good morning Sir's.

Taushree: Good morning, come in and have a seat.

Mahesh Chhedi: Thankyou sir

Taushree to Mahesh Chhedi: As you know we are a luxury shoe manufacturing company, we manufacture luxury shoes for Eurpoean market. Tell me how you can help us in improving design of our shoes.

Mahesh being expert in manufacturing and designing of formal shoe with hole in front was jumping with joy inside as Taushree asked question from something he was doing for years and has also got lots of research papers published. But he did not knew that with Taushree ego, he was in for a crazy ride formally called interview.

Mahesh Chhedi to Taushree: Sir, I have expertise in designing shoes with hole in front for high end market.

Word “expertise” hit Taushree hard as no one in this universe can be more expert than Taushree when sitting in his office!

Taushree to Mahesh Chhedi: Tell me five practical design benefits of shoe with hole in front.

Mahesh Chhedi replied: 1. Hole in shoe helps with flow of air through shoes keeping feet fresh. 2. During rains if water gets into shoes, hole can act as a conduit for faster drainage of water. 3. Flow of fresh air through hole confirms there is no smell in shoes. 4. Small perfume bottle can be kept in hole of shoe making shoe smell like a scent.5.Shoe hole can also be used as a small pocket.

Taushree countered: What if insect goes inside a shoe through that hole.

Mahesh Chhedi replied: Shoe has a big open space on top for putting the foot in; insects can go inside shoe using that open space.

Someone replying so straight to Taushree with logic and winning is definetely not acceptable to Taushree. Inside his mind he decided that now at any cost he has to prove Mahesh Chhedi is a foolish fellow in front of everyone. If Taushree accomplishes this today, he will reject Mahesh Chhedi in interview .If not today, Taushree will hire Mahesh Chhedi, prove Mahesh Chhedi is foolish and then he will fire Mahesh Chhedi.

Taushree to Mahesh Chhedi: Have you done a case study on disadvantages of hole in shoe.

Mahesh Chhedi: No

Taushree: Than saying shoe with hole has a feasible design is a foolish statement. I think you are trying to swallow more than what you can bite with this.

Now Mahesh Chhedi knew Taushree does not like his first reply but if he succeed in interview , he may get 60 to 100% payrise. So Mahesh tried to do some damage control.

Mahesh Chhedi to Taushree: You are correct Mr.Taushree but lots of research has been done on shoe hole feasible design and it seems like it works and at the same time makes shoe look elegant.But as you said we also need to look at disadvantages of hole in shoe.

Taushree again countered to Mahesh Chhedi's reply:But you have not provided a single case study and it seems like you are talking in thin air. What if insect goes inside the shoes when you are walking in dangerous area or in water? It can result into a big disaster.

Taushree then looked at Pedaishi Gulam and Chamcha Prasad for their opinions.

Pedaishi Gulam: Mr.Taushree I have seen some research in market which proves that shoes with hole is a good design modification. However Mr.Chhedi has to find solution of problem you just mentioned and also any other problem which may come with a shoe having hole in front.

Taushree was angry on Pedaishi Gulam as he said it's a good design but kept his cool to listen to opinion of Chamcha Prasad.

Chamcha Prasad: Mr.Taushree I agree with you, Mr. Mahesh is talking in thin air without any evidence of design success. I would also like to give you my personal observation that since the day big bang happened to present time, there is not even a single person who has taken birth and is more intelligent then you, with only few questions you are able to prove with evidence that Mr.Mahesh will not be able to make a great Kachra shoe with a hole. However I also see a opening here if you personally look into the issues faced with shoe having hole and guide Mahesh in finding solution to those issues. We should be able to make a great Kachra shoe with a hole.

Taushree to Chamcha Prasad: Mr.Chamcha I understand without me company is not going to run but I also need some intelligent and result oriented people to make our company more successful , but I am highly disappointed with Pedaishi Gulam that even after so many years with me he is not able to make proper assessment while taking interview. I am putting ball in your court, do you think we should hire Mr.Mahesh?

Chamcha Prasad throughout his career never took any responsibility except full-fledged responsibility of boot licking Taushree, so Chamcha Prasad was not going to take decision on selecting Mahesh Chhedi.

Chamcha Prasad to Taushree: Mr. Taushree you are the greatest decision maker ever I have seen in my life, you have never taken a wrong decision in your life. I insist for the benefit of company you take this decision.

Each and every word spoken by Chamcha Prasad was the greatest music for ears of Taushree.

Taushree replied: Alright Chamcha Prasad ji, let's do some more talking with Mr.Mahesh.

All this time Mahesh Chhedi was quietly listening to all the conversations and by now he knew if he want to get this job with good payrise, he just need to make Taushree happy . Additionally he now knew that everyone in this company is just doing "yes boss job" to make Taushree happy and no one care about this company.

Taushree to Mahesh Chhedi: Mr.Mahesh as you can see our team does not agree with you, please give me at least one reason to hire you.

Mahesh Chhedi to Taushree: Mr.Taushree , You have correctly pointed out that good research is not done in this direction and I think lot more work needs to be done in this direction. I have expertise in luxury designer shoes with hole and you are the most brilliant person to guide me to do proper research and implement it for creating greatest luxury shoes with hole.

Word “brilliant” was the magic word which compelled Taushree to hire Mahesh Chhedi and have some more fun running Mera Ego Limited. Taushree asked Mahesh Chhedi to wait outside his cabin so that all the board members can decide if they want to hire Mahesh Chhedi.

Once Mahesh Chhedi was outside the room, Taushree declared that he thinks Mahesh will be a good addition to Mera Ego Limited and then again asked Pedaishi Gulam and Chamcha Prasad for their valuable opinion.

Pedaishi Gulam to Taushree: Sir I agree with you, we should hire Mahesh.

Chamcha Prasad to Taushree: Sir I think hiring Mahesh and making him work under your guidance on developing beautiful shoes with hole in front is revolutionary decision taken by you. This single decision is going to quadruple the revenue of Mera Ego Limited in coming times.

Taushree to Chamcha Prasad: Yes Mr. Chamcha Prasad you are correct but we need to hire one more expert like him. I am still not satisfied.

Taushree to Pedaishi Gulam: Pedaishi Gulam please negotiate salary with Mahesh and please note; I am not happy with you and your team's performance. You are in such an important position in company still I have to micro-manage you to get things done properly.

Taushree here was simply telling Pedaishi Gulam that he and his team members are not licking Taushree enough to satisfy Taushree's ego.

After that Pedaishi Gulam went outside and finalized salary and joining dates with Mahesh Chhedi.

Mahesh's joining date was fixed for next week as Mera Ego Limited purchased his notice period.

Interview of Suresh Rangwala

Pressure was again back on Naukri Bachao Khan, He need to find atleast one more expert. After lots of searching, cold calling, scanning through job websites and abuses from Taushree, Naukri Bachao finally got profile of Mr.Suresh Rangwala. Suresh Rangwala was looking for a job change .Suresh Rangwala had an expertise in designing shoes which change colour as per dirt on it. Which means shoe never looked dirty. It was niche expertise which was highly sought out in industry.

Similar to Mahesh Chhedi ,Suresh Rangwala also refused to appear in interview of Mera Ego Limited citing similar reasons as Mahesh Chhedi but after persuations of Naukri Bachao Khan and possibility of big payrise he agreed to appear for an interview.

Interview of Mr.Suresh Rangwala was fixed with Taushree , Pedaishi Gulam and Chamcha Prasad. D-Day arrived and Suresh Rangwala came to Mera Ego Limited office 15 minutes before interview. He was greeted by Naukri Bachao Khan; Naukri Bachao also offered him some tea and snacks.To utilize this extra time Naukri Bachao gave Suresh Rangwala some details about the company including company organisational structure. Chugli Kumar was observing the conversations between Naukri Bachao Khan and Suresh Rangwala.

Chugli Kumar got an idea of scoring some browny points at the cost of Naukri Bachao Khan.Chugli Kumar went to the cabin of Taushree to discuss.

Chugli Kumar at the door of Taushree Cabin: May I come in sir.

Taushree: Come in Chugli. Is there anything important you want to discuss.

Chugli Kumar: Yes Sir, It's regarding Interview of Mr.Suresh Rangwala. Mr.Suresh Rangwala has arrived in our office and I just observed Naukri Bachao sir was talking with Mr.Suresh Rangwala about his interview with you today.

Now Taushree was interested, he knew he is going to get good amount of masala to abuse Naukri Bachao Khan and Pedaishi Gulam.

Taushree to Chugli Kumar: Chugli you know transparency in professional life is extremely important if we want to succeed as a company. Tell me everything.

Although Chugli Kumar overheard only few words but he cooked a nice story for Taushree.

Chugli Kumar to Taushree: Naukri Bachao sir was discussing finer technical points and important persons involved who can approve hiring of Mr.Suresh Rangwala .

You mean Naukri Bachao Khan was talking about me? But why Naukri Bachao will help Suresh to clear interview; asked Taushree.

Taushee continued talking: I understand I am the most intelligent and greatest person ever but that does not means Naukri Bachao Khan talk about me with that person.

Chugli Kumar to Taushree: Sir, He is trying to find qualified candidates for company but as you can see it not an easy job to find good candidates.I think Naukri Bachao sir don't want to do the hard work of finding the suitable candidates.So he is trying to prepare Mr.Suresh Rangwala for interview.But Naukri Bachao sir don't know you are the most intelligent person in this world and you will catch him in few seconds of discussion.

Although Taushree knew Chugli Kumar was simply trash talking but he did not wanted to leave a chance of having a fun time with Naukri Bachao & Pedaishi Gulam before conducting interview.

Taushree called Naukri Bacho Khan and Pedaishi Gulam in his cabin to discuss.

Taushree to Pedaishi Gulam: Mr.Gulam how are the things today. I heard your team is working very hard to get best talent available in industry.

Pedaishi Gulam smelled the sarcasm behind those sentences of Taushree.

Pedaishi Gulam to Taushree: Sir, Naukri Bachao is working on it he has also arranged an interview today.

Taushree: And Naukri Bachao desperately wants to get that candidate hired for the benefit of company.Although only one person thats me thinks about the benefit of this company apart from feeding your and Naukri Bachao Khan's family.

Pedaishi Gulam just nodded in agreement with Taushree.

Taushree: Is it for the benefit of company or Naukri Bachao want to close this out soon as he is not able to find many candidates to choose from talent pool.If he can't convience candidates to work under me the greatest manager of all time then what Naukri Bachao can do in this company.

Naukri Bachao to Taushree: Sir, Yes there...............

Before Naukri Bachao Khan completes his sentence, Taushree started shouting at Naukri Bachao Khan.

Taushree at his highest voice level: **Naukri Bachao I am feeding you and your family despite the fact that you are the most stupid & useless person I have seen in my life, you should be grateful to me. But instead of being grateful to me you are deceiving me. You should be fired from the company but your supervisor Pedaishi Gulam don't want to take harsh decision as he is even more stupid and useless than you.**

Taushree to Pedaishi Gulam: **Mr.Gulam, I know you are a stupid , useless and lazy person but atleast keep a good person under you.**

Pedaishi Gulam to Naukri Bachao Khan: Naukri Bachao you see Taushree sir is working so hard to feed the families of each one of us and you are not taking your work seriously. This should go in your KPI (KPI is Key Performance Indicator) and accordingly you should get a pay cut.

Naukri Bachao Khan immediately sensing the problem replied: Sir, I was just explaining to Mr.Suresh our organisational structure that's all. If you want I can send Mr.Suresh Back and look for other candidates.

Although there is no organisational structure in companies such as Mera Ego Limited as in these type of companies everyone ends up reporting to a crazy person.But anyways... lets continue our story.

Taushree shouting at Naukri Bachao Khan: **Send Back Mr.Suresh!! Are you crazy, you want to send him back after wasting my precious time? You are a completely useless person. I don't know why I have kept you in company. Go and send Mr.Suresh for interview.**

Naukri Bachao Khan went out of the room and sends Suresh Rangwala to the meeting room for interview.

Suresh Rangwala knocking the door of meeting room: May I come in Sir.

Taushree: Come in Mr.Suresh, Please have a seat. How is your day today?

Suresh:Good morning sir. Thanks for asking, I had a nice day today.

Taushree going through Mr. Suresh Resume: Suresh, tell us about yourself.

Suresh verbally goes through information provided on his resume and highlighted his expertise of making dirty shoes look colourful.

It was quite a boring discussion and Taushree did not like it.

Taushree to Suresh Rangwala: Mr.Rangwala these things are written on your resume, I want to hear those things which are not written here.

Chamcha Prasad to Suresh Rangwala: Mr.Rangwala I hope you understand our boss is very busy and he has taken out his precious time just to interview you and are wasting his time by telling those things which are already written on your resume and we know.I am sure Naukri Bachao must have explained this to you while explaining the company structure.Our boss is the most intelligent person in this universe and each and every second of his time is precious.The time you have spent in going through your resume and I am taking in explaining to you, In this time boss could have made millions of dollar.

Taushree to Chamcha Prasad: Chamcha Prasad ji, its fine he don't know how we work. Once he starts working with us he will learn how to work under professional manager.

Chamcha Prasad to Taushree: I agree with you but we have to inculcate the good habit of being professional to him right from day-1.

In a nutshell Chamcha Prasad was telling Suresh Rangwala that he should learn to lick his boss right from day-1.

Taushree to Suresh Rangwala: Mr.Suresh please explain how this technology of dirty shoe making colourful shoe works.

Suresh Rangwala: We put neon coating on shoe in a particular style which makes it look colourful when shoe is not clean.I have an expertise in putting this type of neon coating on shoes.

Taushree was thinking that if he asks Mahesh Chhedi and Suresh Rangwala to work together, he may have a wonderfully looking Dirty shoe with a hole. He will also have lots of fun by becoming head of team and abusing Mahesh Chhedi and Suresh Rangwala. But before that he need to confirm that Suresh Rangwala will take his abuses without any issue, in HR language Taushree wanted to check if he is fit to adapt to company culture.

Taushree to Suresh Rangwala: What are the challenges in designing these types of shoes?

Suresh Rangwala replied: One big challenge is appropriate neon coating and design. Dirt accumulated on different shoe might be different and as a result they may look different. We need to make sure even after different amount of dirt on left and right pair of shoe, colour of both the pairs should look same,and this is where my expertise comes in.

Taushree was impressed but he was not having fun. He was still trying to find if Suresh Rangwala is “culturally fit for company”.

On one side Taushree was dreaming of making every rich person wear his trade marked “Dirty Kachra Shoe with a Hole” and other side he wanted to have fun with his employees. Taushree thought why not to have best of both the worlds, let’s check if Suresh Rangwala is culturally fit for company.

Taushree to Suresh Rangwala: Mr.Suresh there is nothing like expertise in these types of shoe designing, I think you are lying.

This was very straight forward counter and with this counter Taushree just wanted to understand if he is culturally fit for company.

Suresh Rangwala replied: Possibly you may not understand how this technique works but you need to give me a chance to see how it works.

So it seems like this guy will not take any shit from Taushree but company may mould him as per requirements.

Taushree asked Suresh Rangwala to go out of meeting room and wait.

Taushree to Chamcha Prasad: Chamcha Ji , you should take a call on this. I am not convinced if this technique will work but still I am willing to give him a chance.

Chamcha Prasad to Taushree: Sir you being the most intelligent person in the universe, if you have taken a call to hire him, we should hire him.

Taushree to Chamcha Prasad: Alright let's hire him.By the way Mr.Chamcha I can see you are putting lots of hardwork in making Mera Ego Limited successful, I would like to give you additional responsibility of improving company working culture. I want everyone in company to follow your footstep and make Mera Ego Limited a successful venture.So I am giving you additional position of "Chief Cultural Officer" of Mera Ego Limited.Some weekend when we are free, I would also like to sit with you and discuss when you noticed that I am the most intelligent person in the universe.Actually everyone in this company should know this.

Taushree to Chamcha Prasad continue talking after a small pause: I hope you have also observed that Pedaishi Gulam and Naukri Bachao khan are not putting their hearts in work this is creating big issue for us.You need to counsel them and if needed other employees of company to make sure everyone puts their heart in work.

Chamacha Prasad immediately knew Taushree wanted everyone in Mera Ego limited to behave like a slave of Taushree and he need to get it done.This was lot of work, but even after doing so much licking and doing so much shit clean work Chamcha Prasad did not got any pay increase or bonus so he tried to push for a little pay rise. Meanwhile Suresh Rangwala was waiting outside on board's decision on his hiring.

Chamcha Prasad to Taushree: Sure Sir, I will confirm everyone is loyal to company and puts his heart in work. Sir, thanks for putting such a big responsibility on my shoulder. I am not sure if I will be able to do justice to the responsibility given to me but I am sure, under your guidance I will make sure each and every person in the team works as per company culture. Sir now your greatness is going in the range of infinity, telling everyone in this company when I noticed you are the greatest person ever born in this universe will definitely inspire each and everyone in this company to work harder.This is a huge master stroke and I am sure it will inspire even lazy dumbs such as Naukri Bachao Khan and his team to work.Sir, Taxes are so high these days' savings are very less for salaried person; government should take some measures to reduce taxes.

Taushree immediately understood that his slave is looking for a pay rise.

Taushree to Chamcha Prasad: Mr Chamcha yeah that's true let me help you a bit by increasing your salary by 10%, this will help you in your savings.You will get another 10% payrise when you inspire everyone in this company by telling them story of how you noticed that I am the greatest person ever in this universe.

With this everyone was happy as Taushree got two persons to abuse, Chamcha Prasad got pay rise and also another promise of payrise when he takes his bootlicking to next level, Naukri Bachao Khan was finally out of the mess of finding new people and also his salary which was on hold was released, Suresh Rangwala & Mahesh Chhedi got new jobs with massive payrise, Chugli Kumar also got a bonus for doing all those Chugli's.

But there was one person who did not got anything out of all this work , that person was Pedaishi Gulam , Anyways when someone excepts slavery in the name of "loyalty to company" he always ends up with nothing in his hands. Moving on to our story...

The RJCW Department

So Mr.Suresh Rangwala was also hired and it was decided once both Suresh & Mahesh join company, a new team will be created. Name of the team will be "RJCW" which stands for "Rangeen Joota Chhed Waala" in English it means colourful shoe with a hole. Taushree will personally overlook the working of RJCW team with the help of Pedaishi Gulam, Chamcha Prasad and Naukri Bachao Khan.

As for branding of shoe, marketing team was assigned to market it. Plan was to get a big social media influencer to advertise it so that everyone should ask for "Colourful Kachra shoes with a hole". With this innovation Taushree was thinking that he will disrupt the shoe market globally.

Finally on date agreed by everyone Mr.Suresh Rangwala and Mr.Mahesh Chhedi joined Mera Ego Limited's newly created RJCW department to develop their Kachra Shoes into Colourful Kachra shoe with a hole.

Mr.Suresh Rangwala & Mr.Mahesh Chhedi's day started with nice greetings by Naukri Bachao Khan followed by small introduction with support staff and company orientation. It was all done in a nice way by Naukri Bachao Khan.

Day 2 of our new joiners was good as well; they completed the human resource formalities.

Fun Started from Day-3 when they started to work in RJCW department under directions of Taushree however their line manager was Pedaishi Gulam. Their day started with Pedaishi Gulam requesting both of them to study all the designs developed under brand name Kachra shoes.They spent first half of the day going through shoe designs of Kachra shoes and Taushree was getting desperate. HALF DAY GONE AND NO FUN WITH NEW JOINEES!!Finally Taushree decided to interfere after lunch time.

Taushree to Pedaishi Gulam in front of whole team: Pedaishi Gulam, What's going on in our RJCW team.

Pedaishi Gulam: Sir, I have asked Mahesh & Suresh to study all the past designs created by us and provide a small summary of our old designs.

Taushree to Chamcha Prasad: Mr.Chamcha Prasad what is your opinion, is it going to help or shall we assign them some other task. We have to bring them to our level as soon as possible.

This was little googly from Taushree to Chamcha Prasad as he did not knew what is going on in Taushree's mind so he was not sure to speak for it or against it.

Chamcha Prasad: Sir, As they have just started with us, giving them some time to understand how things work here will help them getting through this initial phase however we should assign them some more work to make sure they don't become complacent in this phase.But I must suggest that only you have the capability to strike that balance of amount and nature of work that we should give to them. You should advise Mr.Pedaishi Gulam on expectation we have from Rangwala & Chhedi.

Taushree to Chamcha Prasad: I understand your point Mr.Chamcha Prasad, I should sit with Pedaishi Gulam and decide KPI's of both the guys. I get tired of doing so many things but what to do no one in this company wants to apply his brain, I have to do everything by myself.

Taushree although was showing from outside that he is not happy but from inside he was very happy, Rangwala & Chhedi will report to Gulam but Taushree will have all the fun.

Taushree to Pedaishi Gulam: Bring both the new joinees in my cabin all four of us will have meeting. Also ask Naukri Bachao to come for writing minutes of meeting.

Everyone meets up in Taushree's cabin.

Taushree to Pedaishi Gulam: Gulam how is day of Chhedi & Rangwala going on.

Pedaishi Gulam to Taushree: Sir, I have asked both Rangwala & Chhedi to review all our past designs.

Taushree to Chamcha Prasad: Chamcha Prasad ji, you are the Chief Cultural Officer of company and I hope you are taking note that Mr.Gulam is inducing laziness in company culture. Both these guys are starting with us and Gulam is showing he did not prepared for their joining, he is clumsy and he making whole company looking clumsy and stupid in front of new joinees.

It was a very simple strategy from Taushree, abuse the boss and subordinates will get a good idea of company culture and who is the person to lick.

Chamcha Prasad to Taushree: Sir, I think Mr.Gulam has lost it. But as you are here to guide Mr.Gulam he will understand the importance of acting as a professional from beginning.

Taushree to Chamcha Prasad: Mr.Chamcha Prasad I understand when you have a genius to lead the company nobody wants to apply his mind but what is the use of having so many people in company when I have to do all the things.I have to do all the hiring & firing related work, Technical work, decision on shoe design, board meetings, make strategies and on top of that pay salaries to useless people such as Pedaishi Gulam, Naukri Bachao etc. Why I need so many people if I have to do all the work.

Above discussion was going in meeting room in front of key team and new joinees.Chamcha Prasad wanted to play smart to make sure he get some extra points from boss and also not to say anything bad to Pedaishi Gulam as he has to keep good relations with Pedaishi Gulam also.

Chamcha Prasad to Taushree: Sir, Our team is little short in terms of understanding critical nature of our business but I must say under your direction our team has capability to improve and be successful. I think with your brilliant vision and guidance Mr.Pedaishi Gulam will soon learn to take responsibility and work properly for success of company.

Taushree was not very impressed with little flattering from Chamcha Prasad so he decided to give some dosses of his feedback to Pedaishi Gulam.

Taushree to Pedaishi Gulam: Pedaishi so Mr.Chamcha is saying you are very talented and you will learn fast under my brilliant guidance. Do you agree? I think no matter how brilliant a teacher and no matter how talented a student is, student can't learn how to read, write and behave if student is a donkey. In my opinion you are a donkey. You will never learn.

Pedaishi Gulam wanted to give befitting reply to Taushree but he can't as it was not in his nature, over the period of time he became slave of Taushree.

Pedaishi Gulam to Taushree : Sir, I just wanted to give them a little space as they are starting up in our company.

Taushree to Mahesh Chhedi & Suresh Rangwala: So gent's Mr.Pedaishi Gulam has given enough space and you have got your time to understand how company works.Shall we start working now or you guys also need a bed to sleep as an extra space?

Till now reality has already struck both Suresh Rangwala & Mahesh Chhedi that they are dealing with an extremely abusive boss who is not interested in company profit and he will poke his nose in their day to day work and will make their life miserable.His only interest is in abusing his team for his personal pleasure. Further they both also understood that his key team's sole interest is in licking their boss to make him happy. But now they were stuck with Taushree.

Suresh Rangwala to Taushree: Sir, Lots of work needs to be done to create a beautiful & colourful dirty shoe under the Kachra brand. I understand this challenge and I am ready to work for it.

Mahesh Chhedi to Taushree: Sir, I agree with Mr.Suresh. Lots of work needs to be done and I promise you we both will put our expertise and develop a beautiful & colourful dirty shoe with a hole for Kachra brand.

Taushree to both Mahesh Chhedi & Suresh Rangwala: Gents go back to your desk's I will discuss your work profile with Pedaishi and he will let you know.

Both Mahesh Chhedi & Suresh Rangwala came out of Taushree cabin went to coffee machine before going towards their desk.

Mahesh Chhedi to Suresh Rangwala: Suresh, what do you think about our new job.I am afraid I have done a mistake by joining this organization.

Suresh Rangwala to Mahesh Chhedi: Off course, we both have done a mistake by joining this organization. This company is a circus and owner of this company acts like a ring master. I think that ring master's primary interest is not to make money for company; His primary interest is to abuse all the monkeys at his disposal for his personal pleasure. We are just an addition to the troop of monkeys he has.

Meanwhile inside Taushree's cabin, Taushree was discussing way forward for his newly created RJCW team.

Taushree to Pedaishi Gulam: Pedaishi, tell me what is the meaning of name of new department created for these guys.

Pedaishi to Taushree: Sir, RJCW it stands for "Rangeen Joota Chhed Waala" Colourful shoe with a hole!

Taushree to Pedaishi Gulam: I know the literal meaning of newly created department in around three languages. My question to you is what is your strategy to create such a fancy shoes? To me it seems like you have planned to accomplish this work after your retirement. I need faster results!

Chamcha Prasad to Taushree: Sir, You being most intelligent, smart, intellectual, research / result oriented and brilliant person born ever in the history of earth. You can only successfully accomplish this task in best possible manner. I request you to let Pedaishi ji work with them but you should interfere and give them right direction.

These magical words from Chamcha Prasad really enhanced the mood of Taushree and also Chamcha Prasad suggested him way to screw both the new joinees along with Pediashi whenever Taushree wants.Taushree was now happy , but instead of showing his happiness he thought why not to have some more fun with Pedaishi Gulam before letting them go.

Taushree to Pedaishi Gulam: Pedaishi do you see how much Mr.Chamcha Prasad is concerned about the company. My expectation from you is if you can't follow me atleast learn something from Mr.Chamcha Prasad, it will help you to discharge your duties here properly in Mera Ego Limited.

Pedaishi Gulam to Taushree: OK sir.

Pedaishi Gulam goes out of the room to meet both Suresh Rangwala and Mahesh Chhedi.

Pedaishi Gulam in RJCW department talking to both Suresh Rangwala & Mahesh Chhedi: Mr.Rangwala & Mr. Chhedi as you have already heard from Mr.Taushree that we have less time and we have to do lots of works. So let's plan how we are going to deliver Colourful dirty shoe with a fancy hole.

Suresh Rangwala to Pedaishi Gulam: Sir, We should start with doing Neon experiments on shoe design.

Mahesh Chhedi to Pedaishi Gulam: I will start on designing holes from today itself.

Pedaishi Gulam to both Suresh Rangwala & Mahesh Chhedi: Gentleman remember Mr.Taushree is personally looking at this project.

Meanwhile Taushree sitting in room and thinking: its fun to have new guys to abuse, how about hiring one more person as sales manager of these new shoes being developed.Apart from helping with sales & marketing , I will be having one more person to abuse.Taushree calls Pedaishi Gulam, Chamcha Prasad and Naukri Bachao Khan in his room.

Atom Singh:Marketing Expert

Taushree to all three of his key employees Pediashi Gulam, Chamcha Prasad and Naukri Bachao Khan: Gents we need to have one marketing guy who looks at digital marketing and offline marketing for our new range of colourful shoe with a hole. Naukri Bachao and Pedaishi it is your responsibility to get a marketing person for our new department. Also ask Chugli Kumar to provide myself and Mr.Chamcha Prasad with updates on hiring of marketing person.

Naukri Bachao was seriously frustrated now, again he will have to go through same old torture but anyways on same day Naukri Bachao & Chugli Kumar started looking for marketing person.After numerous scans through Professional networks / job sites and numerous cold callings some resumes were short listed.One of the resume out of the shortlisted resumes was that of Atom Singh.

Atom Singh is an experienced marketer with long experience in direct to customer (D2C) marketing.He has a track record of brand building, offline D2C and online D2C marketing. A very clever professional, He agreed to come for an interview with Taushree.

On his interview date, he came to Mera Ego Limited office and Naukri Bachao Khan took him to meeting room in which Taushree, Chamcha Prasad and Pedaishi Gulam were already present.

Atom Singh: May I come in sir.

Taushree: Come in and have a seat.

Atom Singh taking his seat: Thanks sir

Taushree: Mr.Atom Singh, please tell us about yourself.

Atom Singh: I have done MBA in marketing from Highway Management College. After that I joined Phatichar Shoe Company as management intern and I am working with Phatichar Shoe Company for last 15 years. Currently I am marketing manager in sales department of Phatichar Shoe Company.

Taushree was impressed but for him it was equally important to find out if Atom Singh will allow Taushree to have fun with him.

Taushree to Atom Singh: Mr.Atom Singh your profile looks impressive, I have few questions for you.My first question to you is what was the improvement in offline and online sales of Phatichar shoes under you and kindly explain sales strategy you took to accomplish those increase in sales revenue.

Atom Singh to Taushree: Sir, Very good question and thanks sir for bringing up this question in our discussion.

Only a concerned manager can bring up such an intelligent questions.

Although Atom Singh did not give any reply to Taushree's question till now but complement given by him to Taushree was enough for Taushree to take decision on hiring him. Taushree can smell he is getting a younger version of Chamcha Prasad for marketing his Kachra Shoes. But he kept his excitement under wrap and kept on listening to answer of Atom Singh.

Atom Singh to Taushree (continue talking): Sir, due to my strong sales strategy of focussing on digital platforms and working closely with retailers I was able to achieve sales of average 600 shoes per day in last quarter.

Taushree to Atom Singh: Mr.Atom Sales figure of Phatichar shoes are good but as I understand sales are declining for last 6 years after you became sales manager. What was the sales figure 6 years ago?

Atom Singh to Taushree: Sir, you have rightly noted sales figure have declined in last 6 years .With your permission , I must say your business acumen of looking at small details is absolutely stunning. Main reason for decline in shoe sale was top managements decision of decreasing retailers margin for improving profitability per unit shoe .As a result of that retailers were not ready to keep our shoes in their shelf.It was my effort as a marketing manager, I convinced retailers to keep those shoes in their shelf with lower margin and in some cases shoes were over priced also by retailer.

Taushree to Atom Singh: But what was the sales figure 6 years ago?

Atom Singh to Taushree: Sir it was 1200 shoes per day average.

Taushree to Atom Singh: So did increasing the per unit profit margin helped?

Atom Singh was cornered now.

Atom Singh to Taushree: No it decreased overall profitability.

Taushree to Atom Singh: Why didn't you give your feedbacks to your company management?

Atom Singh to Taushree: Sir they didn't listened to me.

Taushree to Atom Singh: Mr.Singh, what you are saying is you kept on giving them your feedback continuously for 6 years and they kept on ignoring you.

Now Atom Singh was little confused if Taushree is thinking that he is incompetent to be a marketing head of his Kachra shoes.But Atom Singh being a smart person understood the character of Taushree very well.

Atom Singh to Taushree: Sir, without beating around the bush you have hit a bullet absolutely on target.This is a trait of an exceptionally intelligent manager. Yes

Phatichar Shoes Limited management were not at all interested in listening to me.

Taushree was extremely happy by getting bombarded with compliments but he was still not getting right reason to justify hiring Atom Singh.

Taushree to Atom Singh: But Mr.Atom Singh if they were not ready to listen to you, why you stayed there for 6 years. You could have left them much earlier; I can see you are an exceptionally talented person who can easily get the job anywhere.

Atom Singh to Taushree: Sir, You have again hit a bullet right on the mark. Yes I could have left them much earlier. But it was my loyalty to company which did not allowed me to leave them, but now I am tired of explaining them same thing which they don't want to listen so I want to leave them for better.

Taushree to Chamcha Prasad: Mr.Chamcha do you have any question?

Chamcha Prasad talking directly to Atom Singh: Mr. Singh as you can see our company has the greatest mind ever in the history of humans in the form of Mr. Taushree , Do you really think you would be able to make difference in company future under greatest guide in the universe Mr.Taushree.

Atom Singh was confused if that was a question or just some more buttering to Taushree, but anyways he just wanted a job and big payrise so he decided to do a little Taushree licking competition with Chamcha Prasad.

Atom Singh to Chamcha Prasad: Chamcha Sir, I agree with on one account that owner of this company has greatest brain in the universe and among the any living thing ever born in this universe. I believe we all are lucky that this super man with greatest brain in the universe is ready to guide us with his super human intelligence in making this company and all of us successful. For myself I see greatest opportunity in my life to follow this super intelligent human, I would follow him, learn from him and make sure sales of Kachra shoes reaches new heights.

This was enough for Taushree , Alright accepted Atom Singh is failure as Sales man but who cares.Even if he is a failure as a sales man but he would be great “Culture Manager” under great “Chief Cultural Officer “ of Company Mr.Chamcha Prasad. No more questions to Atom Singh, He needs to be hired right away. Infact he should be joining Mera Ego Limited next morning, but that, means Mera Ego Limited needs to purchase his notice period and arrange for his accommodation immediately .This is not an issue Mera Ego Limited has lots of money to waste.

Taushree to Atom Singh: Mr. Singh you please wait outside.

After Atom Singh went outside Taushree declared to the team that he wants to hire Atom Singh at any cost.

Taushree to Team: Gents I have made up my mind, Atom Singh will be a great fit for our company. Pedaishi Gulam and Mr. Chamcha Prasad, Please give your opinion.

Pedaishi Gulam to Taushree: Sir, as you are saying he is good I agree he is good.

Chamcha Prasad to Taushree: Sir, I must say I have not seen a human in my life that is better then you in understanding person's behaviour, you can read through persons mind and intelligence. Yes I also agree we should hire him.

Taushree to Chamcha Prasad: Mr.Chamcha Prasad, you can see how much time and money I am putting in making this company successful and I can see you are also putting serious amount of hardwork in trying to make this company successful.I am sure we will be successful in doing so soon as we have just got a gem of person in Atom Singh.But issue I see here is we also have people like Pedaishi Gulam , Naukri Bachao Khan and others who don't want to learn from their past mistakes. You need to improve these guys also; you should inculcate the culture of hardwork (read slavery & boot licking) in them.

Taushree to Chamcha Prasad (continue talking after small pause): Keeping this in mind I have decided that apart from Marketing managers post , I will give Atom

Singh extra responsibility of Cultural Manager of company reporting to you.

Although Chamcha Prasad didn't like Atom Singh as Atom Singh was directly giving him competition in licking boots of Taushree but with heavy heart he accepted it. Anyways Chamcha Prasad was good for nothing but still he went on to become director of company just by licking Taushree so one thing was sure Atom Singh might get his promotions and pay raises soon even if he fails in delivering marketing performance.

Pedaishi Gulam went out of the room and negotiated a hefty pay package with Atom Singh and also made sure Atom Singh joins them from next day by paying huge price for his notice period.

RJCW Team: Up & Running

Next Morning Mera Ego Limited office: All three new joiners were present. As usual Naukri Bachao Khan took Atom Singh to HR department finalised all the formalities and introduced him to complete team of Mera Ego Limited. Today Naukri Bachao Khan was very happy as hiring for RJCW department is finished something for which he was getting good amount of shit from Boss.

Finally Naukri Bachao Khan introduced Atom Singh to RJCW department and his two technical colleagues Mahesh Chhedi & Suresh Rangwala. After introduction Naukri Bachao Khan left all three guys alone waiting for Padeishi Gulam and Chamcha Prasad to assign some work to them.

Atom Singh to both Mahesh Chhedi & Suresh Rangwala: Hello friends, how is the work in office?

Mahesh Chhedi to Atom Singh: Work is very nice, we are enjoying every moment here (looks like Mahesh Chhedi did not want to open up with Atom Singh).

Atom Singh to both Mahesh Chhedi & Suresh Rangwala: I can understand, what is your assessment of owner of company.Is he nice with you?

Atom Singh was trying to get some spicy words but both Mahesh Chhedi and Suresh Rangwala were cautious.

Suresh Rangwala to Atom Singh: No he is a good person , you will see this with passage of time.

Mahesh Chhedi to both Atom Singh and Suresh Rangwala (Sarcastically speaking): Yes Taushree sir is very nice and humble person!

Atom Singh knew were Mahesh Chhedi is going but he showed his indifference to Mahesh Chhedi's comments.

Atom Singh to Both Mahesh Chhedi & Suresh Rangwala (trying to dig more): Yes I heard Taushree sir is very nice and professional person. He seems to be the very intelligent person also.

Suresh Rangwala to Atom Singh: Yes Mr.Taushree is an exceptionally intelligent person; ask Mr.Chamcha Prasad he will tell you in details!

Atom Singh was little disappointed as he was not getting any interesting stuff from both the Mahesh Chhedi & Suresh Rangwala however he was in same department with them so he knew he will be interacting a lot with both so perhaps he will get interesting masala later on.

Atom Singh to Mahesh Chhedi: Mahesh I have heard a lot about your expertise in making fancy shoes with hole. What technique you use to create shoes with hole.

Mahesh Chhedi to Atom Singh (uninterested): You will come to know when you work with us.

Atom Singh to both Mahesh Chhedi and Suresh Rangwala: I am going for a coffee, do you guys want to come.

Both Mahesh Chhedi and Suresh Rangwala refused to come for a coffee.

Mahesh Chhedi to Suresh Rangwala: So we have a new joinee in sales also. Interestingly product is not even ready. But anyways let's see.

Meanwhile Atom Singh was having Coffee and Chamcha Prasad saw him and hence he came to coffee machine to talk with Atom Singh.

Chamcha Prasad to Atom Singh: Mr.Singh how is your day going on.

Atom Singh to Chamcha Prasad: Sir, extremely happy. I am feeling privileged to be a part of most talented team in industry managed by greatest managers ever.

Chamcha Prasad to Atom Singh: Yes, we have very talented team in form of Mahesh, Suresh, Naukri Bachao & Mr.Padaishi. I also agree we are managed by a very talented manager.

Atom Singh to Chamcha Prasad: Sir, you forgot to take your name and in my opinion you are one of the most talented person available in industry.

Chamcha Prasad to Atom Singh: Mr.Singh normally I don't take boot licking seriously but as you are my friend, this time I accept it from you. Taushree sir, has prediction for you that you will also become a good culture manager of company.

Atom Singh to Chamcha Prasad:I was not licking . I just told you the truth; it is my feeling for you.

Chamcha Prasad to Atom Singh: Alright young man, you will go very high in this company!

Atom Singh to Chamcha Prasad: I just want to learn trick of trades from the best. I can see you are the best so I just want to work under you and learn from you to be the best in industry.

Chamcha Prasad to Atom Singh: Mr.Singh I love the way you lick but I understand the difference between licking and being truthful. Still thanks for all the complements.

Meanwhile Taushree was walking through the office and he saw both Chamcha Prasad and Atom Singh talking so he joined in to check what they were discussing.

Atom Singh & Chamcha Prasad politely greeted Taushree: Hello Sir!

Taushree to Chamcha Prasad: Mr.Chamcha looks like you have already started to explain our new joinee on expectations we have from him.

Chamcha Prasad to Taushree (with Atom Singh silently observing): Yes Sir, We were discussing that Mera Ego Limited has the most talented team in industry and all the credit of creating such a good team goes to Mr.Taushree. Without you creating such a great team is not possible.

Atom Singh intervenes and start talking to Taushree: Yes Sir, The amount of understanding you have of human behaviour is exceptional. I consider current earthling's lucky people that you are sharing same planet with them.

Taushree was happy hearing Atom Singh's words but he wanted to abuse someone so he called Mahesh Chhedi and Suresh Rangwala in the coffee room also.

Now Taushree ,Chamcha Prasad , Atom Singh , Mahesh Chhedi and Suresh Rangwala were in coffee room having coffee with casual discussion.

Taushree talking: Mr.Chhedi & Mr.Rangwala , As you can see you have a new team member in RJCW department and your new team member seems to be very smart person. I think you both must have also started your work to sky rocket revenue of RJCW department.

Mahesh Chhedi to Taushree : Yes sir we are working on it.

Taushree to Mahesh Chhedi: Please explain to Mr.Atom Singh what you have done till now.

Mahesh Chhedi to Everyone: I have started to design shoe holes, currently I am working on two designs as Circular holes & Rectangular hole.

Suresh Rangwala to Everyone:I have started to work on different dirt variables. Currently I am working on white sand dirt on shoe and Dog poop on shoes.

Atom Singh intervenes and starts talking to Taushree: Sir, such a straight forward question! Only a great manager can ask.I don't understand why government has not given you honorary position.I think we should ask government to call you "Taushree the great".

"TAUSHREE THE GREAT"!!! Chamcha Prasad was crazy inside, Chamcha Prasad went it to deep thinking "I guess this guy will take my position, I should be careful of him and should try to get him fired from company as soon as possible.

Chamcha Prasad to Atom Singh: Mr.Singh!!! What are you talking about there are numerous greats in known human history, how can Mr.Taushree be just a one of great among so many greats. Look at Mr.Taushree (Taushree proudly looking towards the roof in extreme happiness).Mr.Taushree is greatest human ever in known human history since first human like thing we call Neanderthal walked the earth around 200,000 years ago.

Chamcha Prasad and Atom Singh had started a competition of bootlicking which has crossed all the limits but as usual Taushree loved it.

One thing is for sure, if owner of company is Taushree than bootlicking can make anyone extremely successful (except company itself).

Objective of Taushree to abuse someone was still not accomplished so he calls coffee boy who made coffee for Taushree.

Taushree to Coffee boy: Did you put sugar in coffee.

Coffee boy to Taushree: Yes sir, one spoon.

Taushree to coffee boy: But I take two spoons in my coffee and you are here for long enough time to know this. Your salary will be deducted by 10% for this mistake.

Taushree to Chamcha Prasad: Mr.Prasad you see our company is full of foolish & lazy people right from bottom to top.I am relying on you to correct this.You are free to fire anyone who you feel is misfit in company and is not going to improve , off course after my approval.

Chamcha Prasad to Taushree: Mr.Taushree I agree with you that we need to work on improving team attitude and company culture here, you have acted like a statesman in taking such a brave decision. I appreciate the revolutionary decision taken by you in this respect. I will make sure we accomplish this. Only the great entrepreneur like you can take such a decisive decision.

With this Taushree was again looking at roof but this time he was feeling like he will break the roof and reach the heaven in happiness. Till now company had only one bootlicker but now there are two. A perfect recipe for disaster.

Taushree to Chamcha Prasad: Mr.Prasad I am working hard and putting lots of efforts from my extremely busy schedule just to make sure we succeed but I don't observe such a high amount of zeal in our employees. I only see passion to make company successful in you and now also Atom Singh. New joinees are still not upto the mark.

Chamcha Prasad to Taushree: As Mr.Atom is also having additional responsibility of culture manager of company, why not to make him incharge of improving culture of RJCW department.This department has only two members apart from Atom, and it's a small responsibility which he will be able to take.

Taushree to Chamcha Prasad: Ok Mr.Prasad but kindly review every week.I need Chhedi and Rangwala to get mixed in our company culture as soon as possible.

Atom Singh to Both Taushree & Chamcha Prasad: Sir, I will make sure both Suresh Rangwala & Mahesh Chhedi gets blended into company culture.

After this conversation over coffee, everyone leaves for their work.There was a mental tussle going on between Chamcha Prasad and Atom Singh. To maintain his position in company Chamcha Prasad may try to get Atom Singh fired and for fast growth Atom Singh may prove himself better than Chamcha Prasad in front of Taushree.

Atom Singh went back to RJCW department along with Mahesh Chhedi & Suresh Rangwala and our culture manager starts his orientation session.

Atom Singh to Both Mahesh Chhedi & Suresh Rangwala: Gents, from where do we start.

Mahesh Chhedi to Atom Singh: Atom see I am expert in making nice holes in shoes but not in licking some ones shoes.I am also not interested in having a new expertise of shoe licking, I am happy with Shoe holes.

Atom Singh to Mahesh Chhedi: But if you want to stay in this company, get salary on time and also apply your expertise of fancy hole in shoes in this company than you have to learn this new expertise. As much as I understand management of this company is more interested in shoe licking expertise than Shoe with hole or dirty shining shoes.

Suresh Rangwala to Atom Singh: Atom, if possible you handle this from our side.

Chugli the trouble maker

Chugli Kumar enters RJCW department to check what is going on with RJCW team (Mahesh Chhedi , Atom Singh & Suresh Rangwala)

Chugli Kumar to RJCW team: Gents, how is your work on shoe development going on.

Atom Singh to Chugli Kumar: Mr.Chugli , how is your day. I heard from Mr. Chamcha Prasad that you are one the brightest mind in this company and you can help us with anything we need.

Chugli Kumar to Atom Singh: Yes, but as of now I just want updates on work you guys are doing.

Atom Singh to Chugli Kumar: Ok. I can understand you need to do some backbiting. Actually we all are chilling as of now

Chugli Kumar did not liked his way of talking so he left them alone waiting for right time to do chugli to Taushree.

Atom Singh knew Chugli will eventually go to Taushree so he asked Mahesh Chhedi & Suresh Rangwala to send updates of their work on email to Taushree , Chamcha Prasad and Pedaishi Gulam. Atom Singh also send his work updates to same team.

Evening time, before leaving office Chugli Kumar goes to meet Taushree in his cabin to do that thing which made him best performer in company.

Chugli Kumar to Taushree: May I come in sir.

Taushree to Chugli Kumar: Chugli come in and tell me what going on in office.

Chugli Kumar to Taushree: Sir, Today I was taking notes of work going on in RJCW.

Taushree to Chugli Kumar: Chugli tell me what those three gentlemen did today.

Chugli Kumar did not knew that all three members of RJCW have send their progress report to Taushree.

Chugli Kumar to Taushree : I observed them whole day , they were chatting and they were not at all working.

Taushree to Chugli Kumar: But did you tried to hear what they were talking about, perhaps they were chatting about work.

Chugli Kumar to Taushree: No sir, they were not talking about work.

Taushree calls whole of the RJCW team in his cabin.

Taushree to RJCW team: Gents, please give updates on what you did today.

Mahesh Chhedi to Taushree: Sir, I finalised the design of round hole in front portion of shoe.

Suresh Rangwala to Taushree : Sir , I finalised dog poop colour merging on shoes today.

Atom Singh to Taushree : Sir, I worked on devising offline marketing strategy in the day time later on in evening I worked with Chhedi & Rangwala for their cultural orientation.Sir one thing is great in this company , we always have someone to entertain us. Whole day whenever we started to feel tired of working Mr.Chugli Kumar came to our department to discuss various non work related things.

WHAT CHUGLI WAS DISTURBING THESE GUYS WHOLE DAY? Although Taushree used to love Chugli Kumar but this time Chugli was on wrong side of gullible Taushree.Anyways why to leave a chance of abusing Chugli.Taushree loves variety even in abusing his team.

Taushree to Chugli Kumar: Chugli ,is it true . You were disturbing them whole day.

Chugli Kumar:aaaaummm.....

Before Chugli Kumar comes out of the shock, Taushree started the thing he loves to do.

Taushree to Chugli Kumar (in loud voice):**Chugli do you have any idea, how much I have spend on creating this RJCW department.I am working on a vision of creating greatest dirty shoe with hole in it and you are wasting my time and my teams time in doing these petty Chugli.You are such useless failed**

guy , whom I am just keeping for reasons only god knows.

Taushree calls finance manager Mota Rancho: Mr.Mota Rancho, please deduct 20% from Chugli Kumar's salary this month for creating nuisance in office.

Taushree hungs up phone and shouts at Chugli Kumar: **Chugli get out of my room now!**

This hit Chugli Kumar hard, but now he knew he is dealing with equally smart asshole Atom Singh.Chugli Kumar in his mind decided to screw up Atom Singh whenever he gets chance.On the otherhand Taushree loved it, everyone loves variety and thanks to Atom Singh, Taushree got the chance of abusing Chugli Kumar. But Taushree was little worried also; there is a saying "Never kill the messenger". Did Taushree just killed the messenger itself? Chugli Kumar was always a great source of Chugli for Taushree, but will Chugli Kumar is going to deliver Chugli from now onwards? These questions were killing Taushree, but only time will tell if he killed the messenger itself or not!

Next day all three new joinees had a meeting in RJCW department and they decided to work in best possible way to achieve the objective.They decided that they will keep Taushree, Chamcha Prasad and Padeishi Gulam in each and every update of their work .They also decided that they need to keep Chugli Kumar at bay and Naukri Bachao Khan could be a good friend if he don't try to mess with them.

The Presentation

One week went by Mahesh Chhedi & Suresh Rangwala Created their respective first design as a proof of concept and Atom Singh also devised offline sales strategy as per discussion with Mahesh & Suresh. Now it was time to present it to Top management of company. Taushree was eager he want to have fun with his new recruits.In last one week Atom Singh and team saw Taushree abusing numerous people just for internal satisfaction or just to show everyone " who is the boss". Atom Singh internally among Mahesh Chhedi & Suresh Rangwala called this behaviour of Taushree as "Tau Panti".

Padeishi Gulam entered RJCW room to discuss timing of presentations; Taushree was available after lunch time.

Padeishi Gulam to RJCW team: Gents so all three of you have presentation with Taushree today from 2pm onwards so please be ready.

Atom Singh to Padeishi Gulam: Sir we are ready ,we will be in presentation room before time.

After lunch all three RJCW team members went to presentation room, Taushree , Chamcha Prasad,

Padeishi Gulam , Naukri Bachao Khan and Chugli Kumar also arrived in the room.

Taushree to Everyone: Gents today we have gathered here to see what Mr.Mahesh Chhedi , Mr.Suresh Rangwala and our Culture cum Marketing Manager Mr.Atom Singh has done.

Taushree looking at RJCW team: Gents now floor is yours.

Mahesh Chhedi to Everyone: Good afternoon every one, I will start the proceedings. Last week I worked on creating round hole in shoe.I have created the prototype of shoe for your review.

Mahesh Chhedi presents his shoe with round hole. Taushree picks up the shoes and look at its design carefully. At this moment Taushree wants to find faults in design.Finding faults in design has a dual purpose 1.It results into improvement in shoe design 2.Taushree gets opportunity of doing Tau Panti with RJCW team.

Taushree to Mahesh Chhedi: Mr.Chhedi shoe is looking nice but I think hole is slightly tilted towards bottom of shoes.What if shoe comes in contact with water? Water will surely go inside the shoe.Infact looking at size and design of hole I think even mud can also go inside shoe.

Mahesh Chhedi to Taushree: Sir, to make the hole look elegant we have tilted the hole opening towards bottom but slightly inside the shoe we have changed the angle of hole towards upper side of hole.Nothing can go beyond the point of changed angle.

Taushree was looking for avenue to do Tau panti with Mahesh but it was clear Mahesh is not going to give easy openings to Taushree.

Wow Mahesh!! That was a sharp answer. Exclaimed Taushree. But my friend what about the length of pipe inside opening, this may make shoe uncomfortable for wearer.

Mahesh Chhedi to Taushree: Sir I am working on making it comfortable.

Now Taushree can sense the opening!

Taushree in slightly firm voice:**Mahesh so you want us to eat half cooked chicken.If shoe is uncomfortable , we can't sell the shoe.**

Mahesh Chhedi to Taushree: No sir, it's still work in progress.

Taushree to Chamcha Prasad: Chamcha ji, my butler serves me half cooked chicken and on getting caught he tells us he is still cooking it. Shall I fire him or keep him?

Chamcha Prasad to Mahesh Chhedi: Mr.Chhedi if your shoe chhed is not yet perfect why you are wasting Mr.Taushree's precious time. Do you have any idea, during this time Taushree might be making strategy on bringing some drastic improvement in Kachra Shoes?

Every minute of Taushree wasted by you equates to wasting millions of dollars.

Mahesh Chhedi to Chamcha Prasad: I am sorry sir, but this is the way shoe designs are done in industry.You either leave on expert or discuss with expert at each stage. You have chosen to discuss with us on every stage.

Countering Chamcha Prasad with an opening given to Taushree is a perfect field for Taushree to play with Mahesh Chhedi.

Taushree intervenes and talks to Mahesh Chhedi.

Taushree to Mahesh Chhedi: Mahesh so you mean to say we are disturbing you while you are doing an important work. Or you mean to say we don't have any work to do, please elaborate.

Discussion is surely going in wrong direction and everyone in the room is making his strategy in this situation.

Atom Singh & Suresh Rangwala are thinking of diffusing the situation. All three gentleman's Mahesh Chhedi , Suresh Rangwala and Atom Singh have became good friends and they also understand if they need to survive in this place then they have to smartly unite.

Chamcha Prasad is thinking of getting some points on sincerity from Taushree.Chugli Kumar is thinking of screwing up Mahesh Chhedi, he still wants to take his revenge from Atom Singh et al.

Padeishi Gulam and Naukri Bachao Khan are simply thinking of diffusing the situation. They know if members of RJCW team get fired by Taushree then they have to find the new team again.

Chugli Kumar takes his chance to begin.

Chugli Kumar to Mahesh Chhedi: Mr.Mahesh you are making me feel that it's a lot of work to design such shoes.But I always see you drinking and chatting in coffee room.

This is the moment of truth for Taushree; Chugli just opened a huge avenue for Taushree to do Tau panti.

Taushree to Chugli Kumar: **Chugli don't say that! You are insulting the hard work of Mr.Mahesh , He will get his salary on time weather he spends his time in office or coffee room. So why you want him to work hard?**

Chugli Kumar to Taushree: But Sir, they don't know they are dealing with smartest person ever in this universe. So whatever they do, they will get caught.

Mahesh Chhedi to Taushree: Sir, I am on my seat for atleast 8-9 hrs a day. I don't know how come Mr.Chugli saw me in coffee room so many time. Further Mr.Chugli's chair is quite far from Coffee room so that means he is also sitting is coffee room whole day looking for chugli material.

Nice!! Yorker from Chugli Kumar smashed out of the field by Mahesh Chhedi.

Chugli Kumar to Mahesh Chhedi: You can't blame me for your failure , whenever I pass by coffee room I see you there.

Mahesh Chhedi to Chugli Kumar: And Mr.Kumar how many times you pass by coffee room?

This one is not going as per plan, Mahesh Chhedi not allowing Taushree to do Tau panti and also hitting Chugli Kumar out of the ground.

Taushree to Mahesh Chhedi: Alright Mahesh you put your day and night on this project, but where is the result?

Mahesh Chhedi to Taushree: Its work in progress and as of now it's for management's constructive feedback.

This was a small pin for Tau panti of Taushree, now he knew this guy is not easy to beat so he threw the ball in Chamcha Prasad's court.

Taushree to Chamcha Prasad: Mr.Prasad ,are you observing where this discussion is going.Do you want to say anything or shall we move on to see what Rangwala did last week. Mr.Mahesh is saying he is professional and looking for management discussion!

Chamcha Prasad to Taushree: Sir, I can see how Mr.Mahesh has wasted our time and more then that your precious time.Let's give Mr.Mahesh one more week to work on his shoe design as per your brilliant feedbacks and let's move on to Mr.Suresh Rangwala.

Taushree to Suresh Rangwala: Mr.Rangwala may we see your professional work now!

Suresh Rangwala had prepared well for this presentation but looking at the way Mahesh Chhedi was treated, he knew Taushree wanted to have fun with him also.

Suresh Rangwala started his presentation showing his work on dirty shoes and changes in shoe colour with dirt type.

Taushree looking at dirty shoe: Mr. Suresh it looks like your shoe is still not fully compatible with shit.I am not impressed. It's a very sloppy work.

Suresh Rangwala to Taushree: Sir Colour compatibility with dog shit is 98.64% which is a very good score.

98.64% colour compatibility is a very good score and deep down Taushree was also feeling that shoe colour change is working but he was angry due Mahesh Chhedi's replies and wanted to take out his anger.

Taushree to Suresh Rangwala: Rangwala so as per you this shoe is blending perfectly with shit.If you think so then I am sorry you have not seen good shoes and you have yet not worked in a good organisation. Don't make me feel that it was a mistake to hire you.

Suresh Rangwala to Taushree : sorry sir, I didn't mean that but if you look at statistics related to compatibility this shoe is fine.

Enough for Taushree Alright given shoe is fine but if Taushree is saying its bad then no matter how good a shoe is, you have to say it's a bad shoe. This much is enough for Taushree to do Tau Panti.

Taushree to Suresh Rangwala (in loud voice): IF I AM SAYING THIS SHOE IS BAD THAN THIS SHOE IS BAD. 'No ifs and No buts'.

Chugli Kumar wanted to put some oil in fire at this time just to get some extra point and more then that this is the company culture Taushree has created over the period of time.

Chugli Kumar to Suresh Rangwala: Mr.Suresh I have observed you always seems to say that you are more intelligent then everyone in this company. This is not a good way to work.Moreover it was decided earlier that you and Mr.Mahesh will integrate your designs but we don't see any sign of integration!

Suresh Rangwala to Taushree (pretending to neglect Chugli Kumar): Sir, Alright I will work on shoe design and will come back to you.

But what about integration with Mahesh's design? Remember "Rangeen Joota Chhed Waala" is the name of the project? Reminded Taushree to both Suresh Rangwala and Mahesh Chhedi.

Suresh & Mahesh both reply to Taushree: Sir, we will work on it once our own design is finalized.

As of now both Suresh Rangwala & Mahesh Chhedi were angry with management from inside and they understood that they have made a big mistake by joining this company, but now what? Mistake has been done; now they can only do damage control.

Now it was Atom Singh's turn, Taushree called out Atom Singh's name and asked him what he did last week.

Mr.Atom I heard from Mr.Chamcha Prasad that you are doing an excellent job as our Culture Manager but now it's time to show your work as our sales manager.

Atom Singh stood up and started showing his presentation. Taushree interrupted his presentation in the middle and asked him what his strategy is in general.

Atom Singh to Taushree: Sir, I have started to connect with retailers and also started discussion with some social media influencers.

Taushree to Atom Singh: Mr.Singh this means you have not worked last week.

Atom Singh to Taushree: Sir, I understand your concern, my job profile is travelling & talking with different people, it always looks like to everyone from outside that I am not working. But Sir as you know very well this is way great businesses in retails are established.

Taushree to Atom Singh: I know lot more things also but I think you need to work harder.

Atom Singh to Taushree: Sir you mean I need to talk with more retailers and Social media influencers. Also we have not even touched upon online marketing.

Atom Singh was polite but Taushree was looking for opening to do Tau Panti moreover last week it was Atom Singh who helped Taushree do Tau Panti with Chugli Kumar so Chugli Kumar also wanted to settle his score.

Chugli Kumar to Atom Singh: Mr.Singh but whenever I pass by RJCW department I see you working on computer, when you talk with retailers and influencers?

Mr.Chugli I must say your observation is very in-depth but unfortunately your observations are not correct as you are not capable of understanding how sales & marketing is done. Replied Atom Singh in a funny tone.

Chugli Kumar countering Atom Singh: So you mean to say I don't understand things.

Atom Singh to Chugli Kumar: Mr.Chugli I just mean to say that to understand how things work, you have to work. Only back biting will not do!

WOW! That was a firing reply from Atom Singh and now Taushree has to intervene.

Taushree to Atom Singh: Atom we don't have the expertise that's why we hired you, so let's not get into it.

Chugli please be polite Taushree told Chugli Kumar after talking with Atom Singh.

Going back to Atom Singh , Taushree asked Atom Singh: Atom , So would you mind explaining to us how you are going to market our shoe?

Atom Singh To Taushree: Mr.Taushree Thanks for bringing up this question,I understand your concern we need to put our strategy together as soon as possible to make it a success. Before going on to explain how we market our shoe ,I must say to make this new venture RJCW successful we will need internal support from your side. In my personal opinion you are the smartest & most capable person sitting in this room and we need your support to work and to keep negative people at bay.

This was "Ek teer se do shikar" , Atom Singh made Taushree happy by reading through a small version of Tau Chalisa and He also made clear that Chugli Kumar should not disturb him.Alright Taushree's ego was partially satisfied but still he was not able to abuse Atom Singh properly.

Taushree to Atom Singh: Alright Atom lets proceed to discuss your marketing strategy.

Atom Singh continue to discuss: Sir,My strategy is a three way strategy 1.I am in talks with Retailers for stocking our shoes and we plan to give them better margin than market rate ,2. I have started discussion with social media influencers to advertise our shoe, infact some of them have agreed to wear our shoe with hole covered in dog poop to public places, 3. Online marketing we will work on it also.

Taushree to Chamcha Prasad: Mr.Prasad what is your opinion on Atom Singh's work.

Chamcha Prasad to Taushree:Sir , I strongly agree with one of the point Atom Singh brought out "you are the smartest & most capable person sitting in this room and we need your support to work" , I am still thinking about other points which Atom Singh brought out.

Taushree to Chamcha Prasad: Mr.Chamcha talking to you and Atom is the most pleasant part of time I spend in my office. I know I am the smartest & most capable person sitting in this room and also in this universe but I am also counting on you to support an extraordinary talented person like Atom Singh. Some of the team members are negative about him, lets we all help him. Moreover remember you and Atom Singh are also in-charge of company culture. Both of you have to do some hard work make everyone in company like you.

As a keen observer and a clever person, Atom Singh has realized till now that if he wants to survive and keep these Chugli et al type of guys at bay, he should focus on his additional responsibility of Culture Manager and not on his main responsibility of Marketing Manager. He immediately jumped into discussion.

Atom Singh to both Taushree & Chamcha Prasad: Sir I agree with you both to make each one of us successful first we have to work on improving company culture and make sure each and every employee works as per company culture. We have the greatest manager in the history of mankind in the form of Sir Taushree but still I can see team is not following company culture.Further I must say Mera Ego Limited and its brand Kachra shoes has not tasted the success it deserve just due to the presence of the great Taushree.I guess it is due to presence of laggards such as Chugli Kumar.

Taushree to Atom Singh: Atom you have my full support, you and Mr.Chamcha Prasad should immediately take up this extremely important assignment of bringing each and every company employee in company culture as per standard.I understand just my presence should make this company successful but this is not happening possibly due to execution.We don't have commited employess to execute the work assigned to them.

Taushree was extremely happy with Atom Singh and he went on to give special powers to Atom Singh to help him with company culture improvement.

Taushree to Atom Singh: Atom from today onwards no one can do your chugli and I am giving you special power that you can question any one in company from

Padeishi Gulam to Chugli Kumar if you see that they are not following company culture.

Atom Singh replying to Taushree: Thankyou very much Sir.Taushree, from now on I will spend my whole time in improving company culture and I will not stop till everyone in this company behaves like your slave and only sing Taushree Chalisa.

Taushree Chalisa! Taushree never thought about it, accepted Taushree is paying them salary but this will be next level. Anyways Chamcha Prasad and Atom Singh are only reading Taushree Chalisa but can't make it official.It would be great if unprecented parising of Taushree is made official in the company or possibly salary review of employee may be decided on the basis of praise they sing to make Taushree happy.If Atom Singh manged to make sure everyone sings praise of Taushree, he will overtake Chamcha Prasad in terms of growth in company even before anyone realizes.

Taushree to Atom Singh: Atom go ahead and do whatever you can do to improve company culture.Company culture improvement is extremely important for us if I have to write the success story of Mera Ego Limited. Naukri Bachao , Pediashi Gulam , Chugli Kumar all have failed to do it. Mr.Chamcha Prasad is trying his best to achieve it but still not successful.Now onus is on you to get this done. I am putting all the burden on your young shoulder.

Day was finished,ultimate result of this discussion was zero but one point was clear to RJCW team “Make Taushree Happy” if you want to survive in Mera Ego Limited , Praise Taushree like a crazy if you want to thrive in company and finally make everyone praise Taushree if you want to survive , thrive and grow in the company.

Making good shoe is a secondary job, shoe making can be done in your free time, once you you get tired of praising Taushree.

Atom Singh vs Chamcha Prasad

Next morning RJCW department: Atom Singh, Mahesh Chhedi & Suresh Rangwala having informal discussion among each other.

Atom Singh: Gents One thing is very clear, this company is not interested in our work, their only interest is in licking and praising Taushree.

Suresh Rangwala: I am really surprised , it looks like everyone in this company is massaging the ego of one person and no one is working.Still this company is working and earning its revenue.

Atom Singh: Its simple, they are in good market so they are earning whatever they can earn but they could have done much much better then what they are doing now.

Mahesh Chhedi: Yesterday I felt Taushree was only trying to show that we are fool and he is super intelligent.

Atom Singh: He wants everyone to lick him and message was clear "if you want to survive & flourish here than LICK".

Suresh Rangwala: Now what should we do? We quit our well established job to join this company and now we are stuck here.

Atom Singh: You both do your jobs and lick Taushree whenever you get chance, I will take full time responsibility as culture manager and try to manage boss and his chamcha's.

Mahesh Chhedi: Alright agreed, the way you are licking Taushree.You need to be very carefull, everyone in this company wants you to get fired.Suresh, I hope you also agree with this.

Agreed. Replied Suresh Rangwala in affirmation.

After that Mahesh Chhedi and Suresh Rangwala started to work on project in their hand, whereas Atom Singh went out to do a casual round of office just to check what everyone is doing.

Atom observed Chugli Kumar was pretending to work but from list of open windows in machine, dating website window was open. Then he saw Naukri Bachao Khan was desperately calling someone to get some work done.

Padeishi Gulam was sitting in his cabin; it appeared that he is focussing on his computer. Atom Singh stopped in front of Padeishi Gulam cabin for a small Chat.

Atom Singh to Padeishi Gulam: Good morning sir.

Padeishi Gulam to Atom Singh: Good morning Atom, whats going on?

Atom Singh to Padeishi Gulam: Just working on my marketing and culture improvement strategy.You look so busy today.

Padeishi Gulam to Atom Singh: Yes Atom, lots of work. Extremely busy!

All this time Atom Singh was looking at glasses of Padeishi Gulam trying to see what's going on in his laptop. Through Padeishi Gulam's Glasses Atom Singh observed some youtube video running, definitely Padeishi Gulam was not working.

It is very clear no one is working in this company and whole company has taken up the full time job of making Taushree happy , thought Atom Singh before moving on to Chamcha Prasad's cabin.

Atom Singh stopped by Chamcha Prasad's cabin to say quick hello and tell him that he will look at cultural aspects of company.

Atom Singh to Chamcha Prasad: Good morning Chamcha Sir.

Chamcha Prasad to Atom Singh: Good morning Atom Singh, what going on?

Atom Singh to Chamcha Prasad: Sir, looking at office to see from where to start our company culture improvement work.You are the best man to guide me on where to start our culture improvement work.Your intelligence and experience of working in this company will be very handy for us to accomplish this.

Chamcha Prasad to Atom Singh: Atom as a starting point we have to make sure everyone should be loyal to company and company owner.

Atom Singh to Chamcha Prasad: Chamcha Sir, you are a visionary.I was thinking from where to start but you are crystal clear in your mind on how to improve company culture.

Chamcha Prasad to Atom Singh: Atom I know my capabilities, licking me is not going to help you.

Aton Singh to Chamcha Prasad: Sir I am not licking , I just wanted to share my thoughts about you.I feel, I am the luckiest person in this world who got the chance to work with you.I will learn a lot from you.

Chamcha Prasad to Atom Singh: Ha Ha Ha.. Just in this world or whole universe? Atom you are a very skill full person who will grow very fast in this company, but please don't brush up your skills on me. Let's go together and meet Mr.Taushree, there you will get lots of avenue to brush up your skills.

Both Chamcha Prasad and Atom Singh went to Taushree's cabin to meet him.

Chamcha Prasad & Atom Singh on Taushree's cabin door: Good morning sir.

Taushree replying to both: Good morning Gents, how is your day so far.

Chamcha Prasad to Taushree: Day so far is going great. Atom came to my cabin to seek guidance on culture improvement in company, as he is starting up to take responsibilities I thought to bring him up to you to discuss our strategy of company culture improvement. After all you are the greatest strategy builder in this company.

Taushree was keenly listening to Chamcha Prasad and was feeling extremely happy from inside after hearing Chamcha Prasad's words on his strategy making abilities but all of a sudden Atom Singh interrupted.

Atom Singh interrupting Chamcha Prasad: Greatest strategy builder in the company only? Sorry sir, I don't agree with you.Sir Taushree the great is the greatest strategy builder ever in the whole universe.

Taushree to both Chamcha Prasad & Atom Singh: Sure gents I am always present to help you and your team.I know you both will drastically improve company culture under my guidance.

Chamcha Prasad to Taushree: Mr.Taushree we all are blessed to work under you, who is one of the greatest manager every in the history of universe.

Now Taushree was flying on seventh heaven in happiness and it was a good effort by both Chamcha Prasad and Atom Singh , at this moment Atom Singh decided to further up his game and make sure Taushree goes from seventh heaven to out of solar system directly.

Atom Singh to Chamcha Prasad: Chamcha Sir, Taushree sir is so great if he could have been in United Kingdom he might have got knighthood and instead of Mr.Taushree we might be pronouncing him as Sir.Taushree the great, Infact if you noticed , I pronounced him Sir Taushree the great.

Sir.Taushree the great, Now Taushree was really out of solar system floating in intergalactic space.This also made Taushree think that he has so much money to throw if somehow he gets knighthood that will great boost to his ego.Although Taushree thinks that he is the smartest person in this world but in reality he is a rich stupid businessman who wants to keep his ego high under all conditions and due to this habit of Taushree both his company Mera Ego limited and its key brand Kachra Shoes are going down the drain.

But now the major issue which was going on in Mr.Chamcha Prasad's mind was Atom Singh is too smart what if he overtakes Chamcha Prasad. So now Chamcha Prasad went one more level in licking Taushree..

Chamcha Prasad to Atom Singh: Atom what are you talking Knighthood to Sir.Taushree, his intelligence level is already way above any knight in the history of world.

Now this is too much from Chamcha Prasad. Chamcha Prasad gave Taushree booster to travel within intergalactic space to Sagittarius A Black hole in the centre of Milkyway, but the big issue here is that

Taushree with his egoistic attitude may permanently get sucked in black hole never to come back. So now Chamcha Prasad and Atom Singh need to stop this shoe licking competition.

However Taushree loved it as usual and he wanted them to continue, Atom Singh at this moment played smart and decided to make use of higher then light velocity of Taushree's ego and direct him towards Chugli Kumar.

Atom Singh to Chamcha Prasad: Chamcha Sir, we need to work very hard to improve company culture. You see I was passing by Chugli Kumar's office today morning and I saw dating and chating site window open in his computer although he was pretending to work also.

Taushree to Atom Singh: Atom you mean to say Chugli was doing online dating and chating during office time.

Atom Singh to Taushree: Unfortunately yes sir.

Taushree immediately called Chugli Kumar and asked him to come to his cabin.

Chugli Kumar on Taushree's cabin door: May I come in Sir.

Taushree looking at Chugli Kumar: Come in Chugli... Chugli tell me what have you done since morning.

Chugli Kumar to Taushree : Sir , I am working with Mr.Naukri Bachao Khan on red shoe lace project.

Naukri Bacho Khan! The more the merrier. Taushree calls Naukri Bachao Khan also in his room.

Taushree to Naukri Bachao Khan: Naukri Bachao , Chugli is saying he is extremely busy since morning as you have given him lots of work.

Naukri Bachao Khan to Taushree :I asked Chugli to help me but he told me that he is working on Mr.Chamcha Prasad project.

Alright Chugli told Naukri Bachao Khan that he is working for Chamcha Prasad and he is telling me that he was working on job assigned by Naukri Bachao Khan , That means clearly he is not working since morning concluded Taushree.

Taushree to Chugli Kumar: Chugli you know very well that I love abusing my employees if I get a chance and you help me a lot in achieving this, but this time I was told that I need to abuse you. Reason for abusing you is that you are taking salary and not working.Do you want to say anything?

Chugli Kumar to Taushree: Sir, there is a misunderstanding. I was working since morning.

Taushree to Chugli Kumar with some choicest of hindi abuses: **Am I paying you salary for online dating in office? I am going to fire you now but unfortunately I am keeping you so that I can feed you and your family!**

Issue with people like Chugli Kumar is that they are good for nothing that means there growth in company is only based on shoe licking and backbiting. They cannot fight with their boss as it's hard to get a new job due to their poor level of competency. So only option left with Chugli Kumar is to get abused and go back to his seat.

After a good round of severe abusing, Chugli leaves for his seat. But Taushree loved it, now he knew Atom Singh is an interesting person to improve company culture.But again Atom Singh is not working for improvement in shoes sales ,he is only trying to compete with Chamcha prasad in doing full time licking.

After Chugli Kumar left, It was Naukri Bachao Khan's time to get abused.

Taushree to Naukri bachao Khan: Naukri Bachao , Chugli Kumar reports to you. I need to know what you are doing.He don't want to work and you are so lazy that you don't want to check.You have not learnt anything despite working under me for such a long time.Someone has rightly said no matter how much you teach, donkey will always remain a donkey.Domkey will not learn.

Naukri Bachao Khan to Taushree: sorry sir.

Taushree to Naukri Bachao Khan: It does not works like this , No one in this company works without my interference.I am putting your & Chugli Kumar's salary on hold till the time you come up with a plan to monitor Chugli Kumar's work.

SALARY ON HOLD!! But Naukri Bachao Khan didn't do anything. Why to screw him up? No one knows except Taushree!

Naukri Bachao Khan leaves the Taushree's Cabin.

Atom Singh to Chamcha Prasad: Chamcha Sir, I must say you are extremely lucky to have got a chance to work with "THE GREAT SIR.TAUSHREE".He is such a great manager, he knows how to handle any situation.

At this moment Chamcha Prasad was really afraid .This Guy Atom Singh is crossing all limits of shoe licking and Taushree is loving it, I really need to do something to pull Atom Singh back and show him his place.But I need to keep quit as of now.

Chamcha Prasad to Atom Singh: Yes Atom I am extremely lucky to get a chance of working with "THE GREAT SIR.TAUSHREE".

After this both Chamcha Prasad & Atom Singh leaves Taushree's cabin to go back to work.

Atom Singh comes back to RJCW room.

Atom Singh to Suresh Rangwala & Mahesh Chhedi: Gents how is your work going on.

Mahesh Chhedi : Good and what you were doing since morning.

Atom Singh to Suresh Rangwala & Mahesh Chhedi: Nothing just messed up with Chugli Kumar, We need to make sure we don't allow Chugli Kumar to even enter RJCW room. He will screw us at any chance he gets.

Suresh Rangwala to Atom Singh: But why you are messing up with him, he is an old employee of this company. It might be dangerous to mess with him.

Atom Singh to Suresh Rangwala: Suresh take my words, even if you don't mess with Chugli he will try to eat you.Due to stupid boss, most of the people in this company succeed by doing back bitting. Only way to survive here is to make sure each and every back biter in this company loses his credibility.One thing is for sure, I will make Chugli Kumar's life miserable in this company.

In the mean time Taushree sitting in his cabin alone thinking: Atom Singh is a great find, He can help me in getting points for abusing each and every person in the company! But what if Atom Singh becomes good friend of Mahesh Chhedi and Suresh Rangwala, He may try to shield them. Team of Atom Singh and Chamcha Prasad will do great job in transforming my company but I have to make sure there is no friendship of Atom Singh with Mahesh Cheedi and Suresh Rangwala.

Chamcha Prasad thinking in his cabin:I need to take out Atom Singh, He has understood how this company works and he is becoming very dangerous for my own survival in company.But how to accomplish this , Atom singh is too smart and with the amount of boot licking he do its next to impossible to get him fired.

Atom Singh thinking sitting in RJCW department: Do I really need to work or perform in this company or Backbiting & Shoe licking will do the entire job for me to succeed & thrive in this company.Its important to make sure Chugli Kumar did not get any avenue to screw us up but back bitting Chugli kumar also leads to abusing of Naukri Bacho khan and possibly in future, it may lead to abusing of Pediashi Gulam.This is not good. Both Naukri Bacho Khan and Pediashi Gulam seems to be neutral they are just getting screwed up due to others. But they even don't raise their voices.If you don't raise your voice no one will raise for you.

Mahesh Chhedi & Suresh Rangwala thinking: Atom is crazy! His only interest is in playing politics, but let's supports him.

Chugli Kumar thinking: Revenge, REVENGE, **REVENGE** & **REVENGE**. **SALARY**, **SALARY**, SALARY & Salary.

Naukri Bachao Khan thinking: Shit salary again on hold! What to do? Hail Taushree again!!

The Review

One more week passed by and time to review development in RJCW department came again.

Whole Kachra shoes team gathered in conference room to check Suresh Rangwala , Mahesh Chhedi & Atom Singh's work in last one week.

Taushree to Atom Singh: Atom before we start , I would like to see your progress in improving the company culture .As whole team is present they can also give suggestions on how to improve culture.

Atom Singh to Taushree: Sir, in last one week I reviewed everyone's working time vs recreation time and I also worked on finding amount of time our team works on jobs assigned directly by you. I have made some eye opening discoveries.

Taushree knew right away that this is the real masala to start the meeting. He will get infinite opportunities to abuse his team and massage his ego.He was extremely happy from inside.

Atoms go ahead and show me the results said Taushree.

Atom Singh pulled out a graph of time spent by each employee chatting on internet vs time active on computer.He got this data from IT department after getting authorisation from Taushree earlier in the week.

As per the data Chugli Kumar and Pedaishi Gulam were spending huge amount of time chatting on social media.

Taushree looking at Chugli Kumar & Padeishi Gulam: Chugli , I guess except working for betterment of company you do everything. Padeishi you also need to do lots of explaining.

This time Chugli Kumar was ready, He saw it coming due to his friendship with IT manager.

Chugli Kumar to Taushree: Sir, actually I came to know that Mr.Atom Singh was doing lots of bad mouthing about Mera Ego Limited with his friends and this was seriously harming our company image so I decided to investigate. Only way to investigate was using social media chats.

Now happiness of Taushree was at next level, who cares about business when you have two dogs fighting and monkey as an refree.

Taushree to Chugli Kumar: Chugli kindly explain in details.

Chugli Kumar to Taushree: Sir, I was going through company review sites and I found new poor reviews from current employees.As putting bad reviews are banned in our company , I decided to investigate and found most of the bad reviews are associated with Mr.Atom Singh. I was shocked , how someone can write such bad reviews about the greatest manager ever in the history of mankind! Reviews said You are Egoistic , Abusive , Stupid and due to you whole company is busy in backbiting / playing petty politics.

Taushree to Atom Singh: Atom from the day-1 I knew you are a nonsense person but just to help you blend in our company I gave you the role of culture manager. But your one action has messed up the culture of company very badly.You need to do lots of explanations today otherwise you will not stay in this company.

Atom Singh at this moment understood that backbiting from old employee is more decisive than that of new employee.

Atom Singh to Taushree: Sir, I understand your concern, you are such a great manager but still company is not finding success.Your presence alone should have made the company successful.This is something which was lingering me for long time, So I decided to investigate. Sometime to pull out dirt of company, you have to go inside the dirt and I exactly did that. I went inside the dirt to find out who is making dirty comments on our company.

Long Pause.....................

So what did you found asked Taushree.

I found even some company internal employees are doing backbiting on company, but till now not able to find names.. Replied Atom Singh.

Clearly this was not going as per plan for Chugli Kumar.

Chugli Kumar to Taushree: Sir but participating with others in abusing company should not be acceptable.

Taushree thought: Atom Singh is on verge of finding mass company abuser and Chugli Kumar is disturbing him.This needs to be stopped; Atom Singh for sure is future of company.

SHUTUP CHUGLI.. Shouted Taushree. I can see someone is trying to make Mera Ego Limited better place to work for everyone and you are interfering in his work.This is not acceptable.

Whattt... Whyyy.. I gave Taushree so much masala to abuse Atom Singh but he is abusing me again. Thought Chugli Kumar.But for now it's better to keep quite.

Atom Singh was also very clear now that it's a battle for survival.He needs to pull down Chugli Kumar otherwise Chugli will get him fired. All this time Chamcha Prasad was looking at proceedings thinking of finding a right moment to jump in.

Chamcha Prasad to Taushree: Mr.Taushree despite so much odds and fiasco created by these two gentleman's , you still kept your cool and you are working on credible solution.I can't stop myself I must say this is a hallmark of great human being although you are the greatest human ever in the history.

Big Ego massage when Taushree is angry makes him feel extremely good, Chamcha Prasad knew this and he did this at the right moment.

Taushree to Chamcha Prasad: Mr.Chamcha Prasad , I am working day night to feed these people but these guys are only interested in making unnecessary stories.I am the only one who is worried about Mera Ego Limited.I know I am great but unfortunately these people are not learning anything from me.

Chamcha Prasad to Taushree: Sir, They are working with great manager like you.Eventually they will learn! But my current concern is Atom Singh, He is investigating too aggressively to improve culture of company. I think responsibility of culture manager should be taken off from his shoulders for time being.

Clearly Chamcha Prasad wanted to get Atom Singh removed from the position of Culture Manager but Taushree loved every moment of fun he was getting through Atom Singh.

Taushree to Chamcha Prasad: Mr.Chamcha I understand your concern but I can see potential in Atom Singh, He needs time and some guidance which I will provide. Let's keep Atom as our Culture manager and I assure you I will personally groom him to become great culture manager.

Suresh is Angry

Taushree to Suresh Rangwala: Suresh please show what you did last week.

Suresh Rangwala this time instead of showing presentation showed the samples of different coloured shoes as proof of concept; he was hoping that looking at working model Taushree will talk reasonably.

Taushree looking at shoes: Suresh are you sure this shoe can absorb any dirt and still look new.

Suresh Rangwala to Taushree: Currently it's only customised for dog shit, work is still under progress for other type of shits and dirt.

Taushree to Suresh Rangwala (looking unhappy): Suresh its two week since you started on this project and till now you shoe is only compatible with dog shit. Your work progress is very slow.This way everyone will make this type of shoe by the time your shoe design will be out.By the way purpose of making you and Chhedi sit together is to make "chhed waala rangeen joota". I don't see a chhed in this this proto type.At what stage you both will integrate?

Although Taushree was only interested in having fun but this question was relevant, two weeks of work and colour match for only one dirt type finalized.

Suresh Rangwala to Taushree: Sir, I am working on it but in the beginning designing with dirt and shit handling is taking time. With the passage of time we will streamline it.

Taushree to Suresh Rangwala: OK. Show me if it works.

Suresh Rangwala to Taushree: Sir, I have also brought fresh dog shit to show how it works (Suresh Rangwala pointing towards dog shit lying on side of table).

Taushree to Suresh Rangwala: Amount of shit is less if we want to do multiple experiments.

Suresh Rangwala to Taushree : Sir, I have also got a dog from down street with full belly if we need more fresh dog shit.

Now Taushree was happy, it seemed like Suresh Rangwala was talking business now.

Suresh Rangwala started demo of his shoe, he took shoe and rubbed its left side on dog shit. Shit was smelly and everyone was expecting that it will make shoe smelly even if it works.But once shit was rubbed on shoe, shoe released fragrance from inbuilt de-ordouriser and neon outside neon coating also worked by changing the shoe colour slightly and merging the shit completely.

Taushree to Suresh Rangwala: Suresh how it produced fragrance?

Suresh Rangwala to Taushree: Sir, I have added a small cylinder of de-ordouriser.

ADDED A DE-ORDOURISER! Without notifying Taushree!

Taushree to Suresh Rangwala: Suresh no one does anything in this company weather its good or bad without taking my approval. I am feeding this company and you guys with my money so you have to tell me if you plan to do something. Any critical design feature in any company product always goes through the smartest person in that company and as Mr.Chamcha Prasad says I am the smartest person in this company.

Chamcha Prasad to Taushree: Excuse me sir “smartest person in this universe” I think Suresh should be penalised for this so that he don’t repeat this mistake.

Taushree to Chamcha Prasad: Alright deduct 30% of this month salary of Suresh.

WHAT DEDUCT 30% OF SALARY! Suresh Rangwala is now definitely not happy.

Suresh Rangwala to Taushree: Sir, Please get my full and final done. I resign from this company.

Suresh Rangwala storms out of the meeting room and now Taushree was extremely angry.

Taushree to Pedaishi Gulam (at highest vocal level): Pediashi , **TO SAVE YOURSELF WORK YOU ALWAYS FILL MY COMPANY WITH USELESS PEOPLE .EITHER**

YOU CONVIENCE HIM TO WORK AS PER OUR CULTURE OR GET A NEW PERSON TO REPLACE HIM. I AM STOPPING YOUR SALARY TILL THIS HAPPENS.

Message from Taushree was clear, As a owner of company it's my right to abuse my employees and if they resists I will abuse my long term employees who never say no to me.

Pedaishi Gulam rushed to RJCW room to talk with Suresh Rangwala.All this time he was thinking of stopping Suresh Rangwala from leaving Mera Ego Limited if he want to get his salary.

Pediashi Gulam to Suresh Rangwala in RJCW room: Please don't leave, Mr.Taushree was little angry but he will not deduct your salary.

Suresh Rangwala to Pediashi Gulam: Deduct Salary! Tell Mr.Taushree That I am not his slave.I am enough skilful to get job outside but working under such an abusive boss is not possible for me.

It was clear that Suresh Rangwala is angry and also Pediashi Gulam's only interest was not to get his salary on hold so only way out was to calm Suresh Rangwala and then convince him not to leave Mera Ego Limited.

Pediashi Gulam to Suresh Rangwala: I understand Mr.Taushree was little harsh on you.

LITTLE HARSH! Shouted Suresh Rangwala. He was talking as if I am his slave and also what about Mr.Chamcha Prasad, he wants me to get penalised for no mistake of mine.

Mr.Chamcha only talks to please Mr.Taushree ,this is the way he has survived in this company for so many years. Don't take his words seriously. As for Mr.Taushree, we will make sure this does not happen again. Replied Pediashi Gulam.

But you don't have any authority on Mr.Taushree. Told Suresh Rangwala.

If you agree not to leave this company, I will get this promise from Taushree. Replied Pediashi Gulam.

Suresh Rangwala : OK

Till now Suresh Rangwala has calmed down and it's easy to get this promise from Taushree. Although it's well known that Taushree breaks this type of promises at his will.

Pediashi Gulam takes Suresh Rangwala to Taushree's cabin and request Taushree to talk to Suresh Rangwala on this.

Pediashi Gulam to Taushree in front of Suresh Rangwala: Mr.Taushree I had a discussion with Suresh, Suresh will not leave Mera Ego Limited if you promise not to abuse him in future.

Taushree to Pediashi Gulam: If Suresh works as per our company policy / culture, I will not abuse him.

Pediashi Gulam to Suresh Rangwala: Suresh there will be no abuses for you, just make sure to update us on whatever design feature you are working on.

Although Suresh Rangwala knew this promise is nothing but as he doesn't have any job in his hand so he accepted to stay back in company.

Further presentations and discussions were cancelled for the day and it was decided that Mahesh Chhedi will present update on his work next day. After this everyone went back to their desks.

On their desks Naukri Bachao Khan discussing with Chugli Kumar.

Naukri Bachao Khan to Chugli Kumar: Chugli it's getting very stressful, Salaries of both of us are on hold and I don't know what to do.

Chugli Kumar to Naukri Bachao Khan: Naukri Bhachao sir,Company will eventually pay our salaries but more important thing is to get Atom Singh thrown out of the company.

Naukri Bachao Khan to Chugli Kumar: Then again we have to find a new person to replace him. Again same stress and pressure from boss.

Chugli Kumar to Naukri Bachao Khan: But if we want to save our jobs, we have to put Atom Singh down.

Naukri Bachao Khan to Chugli Kumar:Do you really think Atom Singh is threat to our job.

Chugli Kumar to Naukri Bachao Khan: Yes

Naukri Bachao Khan to Chugli Kumar: I am afraid, I have never tried to put anyone down but this time I am with you to accomplish this.

Chugli Kumar to Naukri Bachao Khan: Don't worry you will be safe, we just need to plan this properly.

Egoistic pig & his sycophant piglets

Taushree in his cabin calls Pediashi Gulam and Chamcha Prasad.

Taushree to both Pediashi Gulam and Chamcha Prasad: Gents I am sure you must have observed the events which happened in today's meeting. I was silent and cordial but Suresh crossed all limits of discourteousness. He doesn't deserve to work in my company but I have to say sorry to him as we don't have his replacement. As my management team it's your responsibility to manage this guy and get me a replacement. Further apology given by me to him is black scar on your faces.

Pediashi Gulam to Taushree: Sir, We will work on finding his replacement.

Chamcha Prasad to Taushree: Sir, I was amazed this person is so rough! He has no right to talk with great human being like you in this manner. He should be fired from company along with Atom Singh. Atom must have taught him.

Taushree to Chamcha Prasad: Get me the replacement and I will throw him out of the door. As for Atom Singh let's keep him under observation.

In RJCW room, RJCW team discussing today's events;

Atom Singh to Suresh Rangwala: Man what you did! You should have kept your cool. You should have understood till now that Taushree is not a good person.

Suresh Rangwala to Atom Singh: Before meeting I thought he is a bad person but now I can tell you that he is not even a bad person,Taushree is an Egoistic Pig.

Egoistic Pig! Although situation in RJCW room was tense but this made both Atom Singh and Mahesh Chhedi laugh. After laughing it out both came back to topic.

Atom Singh to Suresh Rangwala: So as you know now that he is an egoistic pig, we all need to be very careful.We should also understand that this egoistic pig has lots of sycophant piglets that go by the names such as Chugli Kumar, Chamcha Prasad and many more. We need to be careful and even kill all of them.

Mahesh Chhedi to both Suresh Rangwala & Atom Singh: So what is the plan now.I have never worked in such an environment.Normally managers are professionals but here its just a circus which is going on and owner is acting like a ring master.

Atom Singh to Mahesh Chhedi: You prepare for tomorrow presentation and let us plan what we need to do.Remember everyone in the meeting will try to screw you up and please be very careful of Chugli and Chamcha.

Next day: Everyone in meeting room for Mahesh Chhedi's presentation on work done by him in last two weeks.

Mahesh Chhedi presenting his shoe with hole to the team as a proof of concept.

Mahesh Chhedi to team: As advised by Mr.Taushree in our last meeting, I have changed the shoe hole design to outside pointing upwards.

Taushree to Mahesh Chhedi: But Mahesh you told us last time that this will create design flaw which may make shoes uncomfortable to wear.

Mahesh Chhedi to Taushree: Sir, My last one week went into solving this issue. Now I have solved it.

Taushree to Mahesh Chhedi: So Mr.Chhedi it was your job to make a beautiful shoe but I have to leave my all important work and advise you on shoe design.

Now Taushree wanted some ego massage so he turns towards Chamcha Prasad.

Taushree to Chamcha Prasad: Mr.Chamcha, You must be observing that my job is not just bringing money to feed the company and its employees but also to advise on technicalities of shoe making. Nobody is doing anything; it looks like I have to do everything.

Chamcha Prasad to Taushree: Mr.Taushree, No one can stand you brilliance, it's only you who has ability to run this company, feed each one of us and do all the tasks at a same time. You are the greatest man ever in the history of universe.

Now Taushree was happy!! But Chamcha Prasad wanted to make him happier so he turned towards Mahesh Chhedi.

Chamcha Prasad to Mahesh Chhedi: Mr.Chhedi , you should consider yourself extremely lucky to have got a chance to work with the Great Taushree, You should make use of this opportunity. You should work hard in learning tricks of trades from the great Taushree.

This was the mistake Chamcha Prasad did! No one can be smart enough to learn from Taushree.

Taushree to Chamcha Prasad: Mr.Chamcha, do you really think he is smart enough to learn from me.

Now Chamcha Prasad realised his mistake.

Chamcha Prasad to Taushree: Sorry Mr.Taushree, your thought process and mind is so sharp that only a greatest genius can learn from you. But still he should try to learn from you, agree no one can catch light but at least one can try to run in the direction of light.

Meanwhile Mahesh Chhedi, Suresh Rangwala and Atom Singh were thinking: Oh God! I can't believe I am working under stupidest person ever in the history!

Mahesh Chhedi again tried to jump in,Thanks Mr.Taushree for your guidance in making good shoes design.

Good! It's an exceptionally brilliant design change. Now please proceed further with your presentation: Replied Taushree.

Mahesh Chhedi to Taushree: Sir, I have not made any power point, we all can review shoe sample.

Taushree to Mahesh Chhedi carefully looking at shoe sample: Mahesh, earlier you told us that outside hole pointing upwards will result into water or dirt going inside the shoe. How that problem was solved?

Mahesh Chhedi to Taushree : Hole is connected to a pipe which goes down and then changes angle to come up. That change in hole angle is revolutionary change which made this design possible.

Revolutionary Change! Only Taushree can make revolutionary changes in shoe design. How dare he used the word revolutionary change. Now Taushree was burning from inside.

Taushree to Mahesh Chhedi: I don't see anything revolutionary here; you just tilted the pipe up. Don't use big words when you have not done anything good, it feels like you are trying to sell garbage under the garb of birthday gift when you use such big words.

Mahesh Chhedi to Taushree: OK Sir.

Taushree to Mahesh Chhedi & Suresh Rangwala: Suresh & Mahesh, I need to understand how you guys are going to integrate your work. One set of design is close to ready but there is no integration. Further you guys are not making any progress without my intervention. I have lot more work to do apart from guiding you guys.

Till now whole of RJCW department knew what Taushree wants so Mahesh Chhedi immediately jumped in.

Mahesh Chhedi to Taushree: Sir, You are such a genius absolutely nobody in this company can guide us apart from you to make excellent shoes.

WOW! Change of gear from Mahesh Chhedi.

Taushree to Mahesh Chhedi: I am getting tired by so much work but yes you are right only I can make change in this company. Keep working on it you will soon learn. Alright you guys work on integration and let's review next week.

Meeting finishes and everyone goes back to their work desk.

Suresh Rangwala , Mahesh Chhedi and Atom Singh discussing in RJCW department.

Suresh Rangwala to Mahesh Chhedi: Mahesh, You were talking like a disciple of Chamcha Prasad.

Mahesh Chhedi to Suresh Rangwala: If you want to survive in Rome, do as Romans do. Only way to survive in this company with that egoistic pig on top is to become his sycophant piglet.

Suresh Rangwala to Mahesh Chhedi (Laughing): Sycophant Piglet!

Atom Singh to both Suresh Rangwala & Mahesh Chhedi: Gents, We have to plan our moves very carefully now if we want to survive, thrive and succeed in this company.I can gurantee you ,every person in this company is looking for opening to make our life miserable in this company or even get us fired.

Only time will tell: Replied Mahesh Chhedi.

Atom Singh to both Mahesh Chhedi & Suresh Rangwala: Despite all odds, we have survived in this company.If we want to succeed then we have to promise each other "No matter what, we have to work as a single unit here and we will not allow people like Chamcha Prasad or Chugli Kumar to succeed by demeaning us".

Atom Singh continued talking :But whenever we get a chance to put down Chugli Kumar or any other person like him we will make sure to put him down.Further to survive in this company we have to keep on praising Taushree.This is the way all the useless people in this company have got their promotion and payrises.I thing is guaranteed, Taushree's interest is more in self satisfaction by forcing others to praise him and less in increasing revenue of company he owns.If we keep on doing this we will definitely help us grow in this company.

Suresh Rangwala: Agree.

Now as all three new joiners have settled well in company.It looks like coming days will be fun in Mera Ego Limited. We don't know if company revenue will increase or decrease as company owner is least bothered about it, But for sure there will be lots of crazy stuff and company culture building, further Chamcha Prasad and Chugli Kumar are not getting good vibes from newly created RJCW team, they will try their best to get this team dismanteled against very clever Atom Singh .Answers to all the above will be in Part-2 of Hail Taushree. Till then Hail Taushree!!!